# SUNNY DAYS AND MOON CAKES

## Sarah Webb

**WALKER BOOKS**

"Life itself is the most wonderful fairy tale."
– Hans Christian Andersen

For Simone, Lola and Rosa Michel

First published 2015 by Walker Books Ltd
87 Vauxhall Walk, London SE11 5HJ

2 4 6 8 10 9 7 5 3 1

Text © 2015 Sarah Webb
Cover photographs © 2015 Hero images / Getty Images
Little Bird Island map by Jack Noel

The right of Sarah Webb to be identified as author of this work
has been asserted by her in accordance with the Copyright,
Designs and Patents Act 1988

This book has been typeset in Berkeley

Printed and bound in Great Britain by Clays Ltd, St Ives plc

British Library Cataloguing in Publication Data:
a catalogue record for this book is available from the British Library

ISBN 978-1-4063-4836-1

www.walker.co.uk

Dear Reader,

Thank you for picking up *Sunny Days and Moon Cakes*. I've wanted to write a book about sisters for a long time. I have two sisters. I'm the eldest, Kate's in the middle and Emma is the youngest. So I know all about being a sister! As teenagers we used to fight a bit, but now we are really close. In this book, Sunny and her little sister, Min, are also very close. They're both from China originally, but they now live with their new parents on a small island called Little Bird.

Sunny's life isn't easy. She has an anxiety disorder called selective mutism and she finds talking to people other than members of her direct family terrifying. She gets terribly nervous and her throat closes up. She only ever talks to Min and her parents. Her greatest wish is to be able to speak like everyone else. Does Sunny's wish come true? You'll have to read on to find out...

It took me a long time to research selective mutism as I wanted to get it right. I was lucky to meet a mum early on who has daughters with the condition and she was really helpful: reading my manuscript and talking to me about her daughters' lives. I also watched a lot of documentaries and read academic books. An expert in the field, a UK speech therapist called Maggie Johnson, was also a great help.

It's amazing how kind people are if you ask them for help with research! Lots of researching went into this book – not just about selective mutism, but about many other things too. I even got to visit Hong Kong and fly in a helicopter with the Irish Coast Guard. To find out why, you'll have to read the book.

I loved writing Sunny's story and I hope you will like reading it.

Best and many wishes,
Sarah XXX

P.S. For teacher's notes on using The Songbird Cafe Girls series in the classroom, see www.SarahWebb.ie.

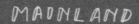

MAINLAND

SEAFIRE POINT

HORSESHOE BAY

SUNNY

LOUGH CARA

BLIND HARBOUR

CARA WOODS

SOUTH HARBOUR

FASTNET LIGHTHOUSE

REDROCK
VILLAGE

PRIMARY
SCHOOL

The
Songbird
Cafe

RED MOLL'S
CASTLE

BULL
ISLAND

LITTLE
BULL

MOLLIE

THE ATLANTIC

N

W        E

S

Little
Bird
Island

# Chapter 1

"Sunny!"

My little sister, Min, runs into my bedroom, trips over the edge of my zebra-print rug and ends up in a heap on the floor. "Oops!" She jumps up and giggles. "Ready for your birthday party?" she asks.

I stop sketching to pull a face at her. "Do I have to go?"

"Sunny, of course you do! Alanna's organized it for you."

Alanna is the kindest person I know and she has always been wonderful to me. She's planned a birthday party for me at the Songbird Cafe, which she owns and runs. I can't let her down by not being there.

And it doesn't look like Min's going to give me a choice anyway. She yanks my arm, pulling me out of my chair. For a tiny thing, she's surprisingly strong.

"Come on, lazy head!" she says, dragging me out of my bedroom and down the long corridor. I almost stumble over one of the loose boards in the floor.

Our home is full of holes. We live in a castle, you see, a *real* castle on Little Bird Island. I know! Crazy, isn't it?

Living in a castle is a lot of fun. The bedrooms are all on the ground floor, along with the kitchen. Then there's our huge living room on the first floor, which has a second-floor mezzanine, or loft, suspended above one end of it. There's also a small third floor that opens onto the roof parapets – built-up walls with wide slots like gappy teeth that were designed to protect soldiers on the roof from being attacked.

Our castle was built in the fifteenth century. It sits on top of a hill, and you can see all the way across Horseshoe Bay to the mainland from one side of the roof and out across the Atlantic Ocean from the other side. Whenever there's a whale sighting, me and Min sit up there with Dad's telescope and watch for their long grey backs.

I wish I could stay in my castle today. I hate going to the cafe in the afternoon when it's full of visitors from the mainland. Being surrounded by strangers doesn't bother Min one bit – she's a right chatterbox and will talk to anyone. I'm the exact opposite. When I am outside the house, I go all quiet. Back in China – where I lived until I was eight – I could speak to anyone, even people I didn't know. But then Papa died and my whole world changed.

I try not to think about the past. I need to focus on my new life. It's hard to fit in, though, when you have no voice. In China, I knew who I was – Soon Yi, a chatterbox like Min, with lots of friends. Right now, I don't know who I am…

# Chapter 2

As Min and I walk down the hill towards the Songbird Cafe with Mum, Min is full of questions as usual. "Will there be chocolate cake? I love chocolate cake. And fairy cakes? And…" She gabbles away, and I zone out until she asks, "Will Mollie be there, Mum?"

"I think so," Mum says. "Alanna certainly invited her. And Landy and Cal."

Little Bird is very small – only about two hundred people live here and only six of them are around my age: Mollie, Landy, Cal, and three other girls called Bonnie, Chloe and Lauren.

Landy and Cal are nice to me, but I wouldn't call them friends exactly. It's different with Mollie. We most definitely *are* friends. She doesn't seem to mind the fact that I can't speak to her. We communicate in other ways.

Mollie is new to the island. She only arrived in February. Her mum's a television presenter and is always travelling, so Mollie is living with her great-granny for a while. I hope she stays for ever and ever.

"Is Cal better then?" Min asks. Cal had a really bad virus recently. He had to stay at home and rest for ages. He's missed loads of school and no one saw him for months. Poor Cal.

Mum nods. "Much better. You OK, sweetheart?" she asks me. "We don't have to stay long, but it would be rude not to show up. Alanna's gone to a lot of effort for today. She wants to thank you for everything you did for the cafe. It would be closed now if it wasn't for you, Landy and Mollie."

A couple of months ago, developers tried to buy the Songbird Cafe and turn it into a hotel, but Mollie organized a campaign to save it, and I designed a Save the Songbird logo and posters. It worked too!

I walk on ahead, not wanting to hear any more about the party. I'm not good with crowds. Even small ones make me nervous. My heart is racing, my palms are sticky and I can feel my whole body getting more and more tense. I try taking a few deep breaths to calm myself down, like Doctor Hogan suggested. Milkshake breathing, he calls it – breathing in s-l-o-w-l-y through your nose and out s-l-o-w-l-y like you're blowing milk through a straw and trying not to make the bubbles go over the top of the glass.

I wish I wasn't so scared all the time. It's my birthday. I should be happy and, knowing Alanna, she'll have planned a terrific party. She's probably baked me a cake too. Plus, she's my friend, and I do want to see her. Along with Mollie, she's my *only* close friend. I'm homeschooled by my mum, so I don't know that many people.

Being the only one in the class can be a bit full on, so whenever I need to get out of the house – and away from Mum – Alanna lets me sit in the cafe and draw. Sometimes I help her in the kitchen – cooking, or stirring her special herbal remedies. I always feel safe when Alanna's around, even though I can't speak to her. If the cafe had closed down, it would have been terrible, for the island and for me. The cafe is my happy place. And I think a lot of the islanders feel the same way.

I'm even more nervous today than usual and not just because of my birthday party.

We've been talking about visiting mine and Min's birth country for years now, but I didn't think it was going to happen so soon. Then Mum and Dad brought it up again a few weeks ago, and this morning they surprised me with plane tickets to China. They said they were a special birthday present, to celebrate me turning thirteen. That's Dad for you – once he's made up his mind about something, it happens, quick as a flash.

Mum and Dad are so excited about the trip, Min too. But even thinking about going back to China makes me jittery. And I don't need to feel any more anxious right now. I wish I could stop thinking about it.

I feel Mum's hand on my shoulder. "I understand parties are hard for you, Sunny. And I'm proud of you for trying."

I give her my best attempt at a smile. It's not Mum's fault I can't relax and act like a normal person. Even Doctor Hogan isn't sure why I'm like this, and he's a top doctor. He's nice, but a bit stern and he wears funny-looking spotty bow ties. He says I have an anxiety disorder called selective mutism, which means that when I get worried or nervous, my throat closes up and I can't talk. I don't choose not to speak – I physically can't.

When we walk through the door of the cafe, I'm relieved to see only a few people inside. Mollie, Cal and Landy are sitting on the leather sofa and armchairs overlooking the harbour. As I walk in, Mollie jumps to her feet, grinning. "Hey, birthday girl," she says. She gives me a big hug, and her fluffy black-and-white striped jumper tickles my nose. "You look great as always. Love the jeans! Are they new?"

I look down at my metallic-silver jeans and then up again, to smile at Min.

"Birthday present from *moi*." Min points at herself. "Don't I have impeccable taste?"

"Yes, Min." Mollie grins and rolls her eyes. "Impeccable."

Everyone laughs. Min's tiny – she only reaches up to my waist – and I think people forget that she's actually eight, not five. She's a bit of a character. People think she's so clever and funny. She's always teasing me, but she's impossible to tease back cos she knows she's a mini drama queen and laughs at herself all the time.

"She got an iPhone too and loads of art stuff," Min adds. "And a trip to China. We're going in a few weeks."

"Cool!" Mollie says. "You're so lucky, Sunny. China – how

amazing is that? And it's great about the iPhone. We can text each other now."

I smile and nod at her. My heart sank this morning, though, when I opened the package from Mum and Dad and found a phone inside. "It's not for ringing people," Mum explained quickly. "It's for all your music and for using the Internet. And texting your friends."

"Thanks," I said, relieved. I felt so bad for Mum and Dad. That was the second time my face had dropped while I was opening my presents. The first was when I opened the envelope with the airline tickets for China. My parents try so hard, and I am always disappointing them. They deserve a normal daughter, not one like me – a weirdo who can't even talk to anyone but them and Min.

"Thought I heard Min's voice," Alanna says, interrupting my thoughts. She bustles out of the kitchen, wiping her hands on a tea towel. Her dark brown hair is in two plaits today, like mine, and she's wearing yellow dungarees under her pale blue chef's apron.

"What do you think of the birthday lanterns, Sunny?" she asks. "Mollie and I had such fun making them." She waves at the red Chinese lanterns that are looped across the window. They're made of a silky material that shimmers in the light.

As I look at them, an image flitters across my memory. *Huge red silk lanterns swaying in the breeze.* I try to hold on to it, to remember where I saw those lanterns, but it's gone.

"Do you like them, Sunny?" Alanna asks.

I nod. Her eyes are so kind and understanding that I feel like hugging her.

"They're beautiful," Mum says, speaking for me. "We had some paper ones up for the Lantern Festival, but these are much bigger, and I love the silk." Mum is very keen on keeping us in touch with our heritage. We always decorate the house to celebrate things like Spring Festival and the start of the Chinese New Year. And now we're off to China, to see our old home and to visit the orphanage where we lived after Papa died.

I turn away from the lanterns and my back stiffens when I spot two strangers sitting at a table near the counter. Birdwatchers from the look of them – they're wearing wellies, and green jackets with lots of pockets. *Breathe, Sunny,* I remind myself. *Take long, deep breaths. Mum's here and Min's here. Nothing bad's going to happen. No one's going to try to make you speak.*

"Sit yourselves down and I'll bring out the party food," Alanna says gently, guiding me away from the strangers.

"Beside me, Sunny." Mollie pats the seat to her right. As soon as I've joined her, she presses something into my hands. "Happy birthday. I hope you like it."

It's a present wrapped in rainbow-coloured paper. I open it carefully. Inside is a beautiful silver bracelet with a tiny dolphin charm on it.

"That's Click," Mollie says. Click is the island's resident dolphin.

"And me and Cal got you this." Landy hands over another present.

"It was Mollie's idea," Cal admits, brushing his floppy black hair out of his eyes.

I smile at them shyly. I didn't know Landy that well until we worked on the Save the Songbird Cafe campaign together and I still feel nervous around him. I'm even more anxious with Cal as I haven't seen him much recently. Cal's mum, Mattie, runs a sea safari for the tourists, as well as working on the ferry to the mainland. Cal helps her out sometimes and he has promised to take us whale spotting in the summer. We went last year and it was amazing.

Landy and Cal are always nice to me. They never tease me, unlike Lauren and Chloe. Thank goodness they're not here today.

I open the tissue-paper wrapping on Cal and Landy's present and find a silver-and-turquoise charm in the shape of a globe, no bigger than my thumbnail. If you look carefully, you can make out the different countries, just like on a real globe.

I carefully click the new charm onto the bracelet Mollie gave me, next to the dolphin one. Then I hold out my wrist and look at Min, who helps me to put the bracelet on. I never have to tell Min what I want – she always just knows.

"The silver matches your jeans perfectly," Min says and then beams at everyone. "We all have impeccable taste."

Everyone is laughing again as Alanna walks towards us, laden down with plates, two balanced on each arm. Mollie and I help her put them down on the coffee table in front of the sofa. There are tiny sandwiches with their crusts cut off, chocolate-chip cookies the size of your hand and finally, my favourite, moon cakes, which are round pastries filled with a sweet red-bean filling. They're Chinese and are usually eaten during Mid-Autumn Festival. Alanna knows they're my favourite thing in the whole wide world and she often bakes them especially for me, with a nightingale stamped onto the top of each one. "Nightingale" is what she always calls me.

My Chinese Mama used to make the most delicious moon cakes for my birthday too. And she'd decorate the whole house with balloons and streamers and she'd draw me a beautiful card. She was a brilliant artist.

"Tuck in," Alanna says to me, gesturing at the plates of food.

I help myself to a moon cake. It's hard to swallow when I'm nervous, but I manage half of it. It tastes almost as good as Mama's. Min doesn't remember her or Papa. She was nearly two when Mama died; I was six. And then Papa died ten months later and we had no one. Ever since I opened the envelope this morning I can't stop thinking about China and Mama and Papa, and it's making me sad.

"You OK?" Mollie asks in a low voice.

I shrug. "Want to hear my new movie idea?" she asks, clearly trying to cheer me up. Mollie loves films. She recently decided that she wants to be a screenwriter or a movie director when she's older. She's always thinking up new plot ideas. With a TV-presenter mum, I guess it runs in the family.

"Movie?" Min pipes up. She's sitting on the other side of me. "Can I be in it?"

"Sure," Mollie says easily. "It's about this girl who can turn into different animals. A shape-shifter. I need to find someone who can twitch their nose like a rabbit."

"I'm a great twitcher," Min says. "Watch." She scrunches up her face and tries to wiggle her nose.

Mollie stifles a laugh. "Maybe you can be—"

"The star, of course," Min says.

Mollie grins and rolls her eyes at me. "OK, Min, you can play the lead." They start talking about the movie and gradually forget about me. Sometimes Min and Mollie include me in the conversation – they are used to asking me yes or no questions at this stage – sometimes they don't. I'm used to that.

They don't mean to leave me out and most of the time it's a relief. Otherwise I have to do lots of nodding and gesturing, or Min has to jump in and answer for me. It can be frustrating, though, not being able to give my opinion when they're talking about a movie I really like or a game I think is stupid.

I catch Mum watching me a couple of times while Min and Mollie are chatting. She has a funny look on her face, but I just smile at her and she smiles back.

After a while, Alanna disappears into the kitchen and returns with a birthday cake decorated with pink and white icing. She places it on the table in front of me with a "Ta-da!" There are tiny iced roses on it and a yellow ribbon is tied around the middle. It's stunning. The thirteen candles are all flickering, waiting for me to blow them out.

I'm a bit overcome. Alanna's gone to so much trouble today

and everyone's given me such thoughtful presents. I play with the tiny Click charm on my new bracelet, running my fingers over its sleek silver back as I think about the cake Mama baked for my sixth birthday. It was a giant moon cake with my name on it. She died two days later. By my seventh birthday, I was in the orphanage and all I got was a cupcake with a single birthday candle stuck in it, a book and a new hairband. I told Min this once and she didn't believe me. She has no idea how lucky she is – living with Mum and Dad, who love buying us presents.

"Blow the candles out, Sunny," Mum says.

I'm not sure I'll have enough breath. And besides, I hate opening my mouth when there are strangers around.

"Will I help you?" Min whispers.

I give her a tiny nod. Together we take a deep breath. I try to pretend I'm at home, doing my milkshake breathing, and – *whoosh* – they're out.

"Now close your eyes and make a wish, Sunny," Alanna says.

*I wish I could thank everyone for my presents*, I think, my eyes squeezed shut. *I wish I had a voice.*

I open my eyes, and before I know what's happening they start to fill with tears. I look over at Min for help and she says something in Mum's ear.

"I'm afraid we have to go," Mum tells everyone. "Sunny's dad is cooking a special birthday dinner and I promised we'd be back to help him."

"But I can stay, can't I, Mum?" Min says.

"If that's OK with Sunny." Mum looks at me.

I shrug and then nod. I know it's supposed to be my birthday party, but Min will keep everyone entertained. She's the fun one, not me.

"Hang on for a second, Sunny," Alanna says. "I have something for you. Over here." I follow her towards the cash desk, where she reaches into a drawer and then hands me a package. Inside is a beautiful red-leather-bound sketchbook with a pocket in the back.

I give her a big smile.

"I'm glad you like it," she says. "I can't believe you're a teenager now. I hope the year is good to you. You deserve the sun, the moon and the stars, my little nightingale." She hugs me. She smells sweet – of wild flowers and baking.

I hug her back. I want to stay, chatting and laughing and having fun with my friends and eating all the goodies. But it doesn't matter how much I want to do all that, I can't. Not even on my birthday.

# Chapter 3

"Did you miss me, Sunny?"

I look up from my desk. Min is standing in the doorway to my room with one hand on her hip. She looks like she's about to sing "I'm a Little Teapot" and it makes me smile.

"What are you laughing at?" she asks.

"Nothing."

She comes inside and closes the door carefully behind her. Then she walks towards me and rests her bum against the edge of my desk. "Can I ask you something? Why can't you talk outside the house? I know Mum and Dad have tried explaining it to me, but I still don't really understand. And you never want to talk about it. I didn't care that much before, but a girl at school was asking me why you're always quiet and I didn't know what to say. Dad said it's none of her business and Mum said to tell her that you're shy and don't like strangers. Will you tell me about it? Just this once?"

I put down my pencil and close the sketchbook Alanna gave me. Min's always trying to spy on my drawings. "I don't like talking about it because I don't know the answer," I say.

"It annoys me too. I'd speak if I could. I just can't, OK?" I start to chew my lip. I hate talking about this.

"Is that why Mum and Dad said I wasn't to ask you? Cos you get all upset? You won't tell on me, will you?"

"I'm not going to tell on you. And I'm not upset. Look, it's complicated."

"Make it uncomplicated then."

I know I'm not going to get rid of her without answering her question, and she does deserve an explanation. It can't be easy having me as a sister. I try to think how I can explain it to her. Then I get an idea. "OK, what would happen if Mum and Dad said you had to sleep in your own bedroom?" I ask.

Min shifts around a little. "Alone, you mean?"

"Yes." Every night after Mum and Dad say good night to her, Min sneaks into my bed. She sleeps there all night. Mum and Dad have tried getting her to stay in her own room, but she won't.

She pouts. "I wouldn't like it."

"Why?"

"You know why."

"Min, that was last year. There are no spiders—"

She clamps her hands over her ears. "Don't say the S word."

"Sorry. The S thing was a one-off. A weird, crazy, freaky thing that will never happen again." Poor Min. She was lying in bed one night when hundreds of tiny baby spiders came parachuting down on silky threads and landed on her bed. Their mother had attached a large egg sack to the light fitting and they'd hatched. I've never heard anyone scream so loudly. She's refused to sleep in her room ever since.

"How do you know that?" she asks.

"I just do. You hate the *S* word, right?"

"Yes!" She nods firmly. "They're evil."

"And they make you feel scared and nervous even though you know they're tiny and can't hurt you."

"They're disgusting. Stop talking about them." She shudders.

"The way you're feeling now, that's how I feel when I think about having to talk in front of strangers." Even using the words "strangers" and "talk" in the same sentence is making my heart race.

Min thinks about this for a second. "So it's like a phobia?"

"I guess."

"Can I tell people you have a talking phobia? Like I have an S-word phobia?"

"OK." It's not a great explanation, but it's better than nothing. "And it's called arachnophobia – the fear of the eight-legged insects that shall not be named."

She pulls a *that's nasty* face and then says, "Can I ask you one more thing? Is that why you're scared of going to China? Because of all the strangers?"

"How do you know I'm scared?"

"I saw your face when you opened that envelope with the plane tickets inside. There are a whole lot of people in China, aren't there?"

I shrug. "That's part of it. But also it makes me sad to think about Mama and Papa and everything. I know this is our home now, but I miss them sometimes. Don't you?"

She thinks for a second, then says, "Not really. I remember Papa a bit, but not Mama. He was bald, wasn't he? He used to let me rub his head."

I smile. "That's right."

"Is it like the way I miss Woody? How you feel, I mean?" Woody was our dog before Goldie, our yellow Labrador. He was run over by a tractor two years ago and Min was really upset about it.

"Exactly," I say.

She nods her head solemnly. "I get it. I'm sorry you feel sad, Sunny. Especially on your birthday." She puts her arms around me and squeezes me tight. "But you've always got me."

She's so sweet; my eyes tear up again.

Later, when Min's out walking Goldie with Mum, I sit at my desk and stare at the large white envelope holding the plane tickets for China. As soon as I opened the envelope this morning, I started to get that fluttery-scared feeling in my stomach and I could feel my eyes blinking fast.

"Are you all right, Sunny?" Dad asked. He'd noticed that I'd gone all quiet.

"I'm just excited," I said. "Thanks – it's a brilliant present."

"Do they have a Disney World in China?" Min jumped in. "Can we go?"

Mum laughed. "Min, we can go to Disney World anytime."

Dad nodded. "Your mum's right, Minnie Mouse. We'll be far too busy to bother with a theme park."

Min looked disappointed for a moment, but she bounced back quickly and started asking lots of questions about what we would do in China.

Mum told her to be quiet. She had a worried look on her face. "Sunny, we don't have to go on the trip if you don't want to," she said.

Before I got the chance to answer, Min said, "What? Of course we're going. It's gonna be amazing. Do you think everyone will look like us? Imagine if someone recognized us in the street or something. One of our old neighbours."

Mum laughed. "It's a huge place, not like Little Bird. That's unlikely to happen, Min. Now, shush! Let Sunny speak."

Mum and Dad were both looking at me, their eyes full of hope and expectation.

"Sunny?" Dad said. "What do you think? Are you excited? We can just go to Hong Kong if you like. We don't have to visit your old home in Shenzhen or the orphanage. Or if you are really unhappy about going, we can stay at home. The tickets are refundable, so there's no pressure on you."

I took a deep breath and said, "Min's right. It'll be amazing. I can't wait."

You see, even though I'm scared, I do want to go to China, and not just because my family are so excited about the trip. I need to see if my vivid dreams of twisted trees and silky grey cats are real or just my imagination. And I'd like to show Min the park where we once played, if we can find it, and my old school. Maybe Min will start remembering things about China when we get there. It would be nice to have some memories in common.

But also, deep down, I'm hoping that something magical will happen in China. That somehow the trip will help me to stop worrying all the time. Then, when I come home to Little Bird, I'll be able to talk freely. I'll be me – happy, chatty Soon Yi – again.

# Chapter 4

Before dinner, I hear muffled voices coming from the floor below. After putting down my sketchbook, I jump off the window seat in the living room and carefully peel back the edge of the rug so I can peer through a crack in the old floorboards. The gap is so large that I can actually see Mum and Dad in the kitchen, standing in front of the Aga. Dad has his arm around Mum's shoulders. Dad's tall and Mum slots perfectly under his arm. They fit together like two pieces of Lego.

I know I shouldn't spy on them, but I can't help myself. I've been doing it for years.

As I watch, Mum rests her head on Dad's shoulder. She sighs. "I'm just so worried about her."

"Don't be," he says. "She'll be OK."

Mum lifts her head. "No, she won't. Don't you see? She's thirteen. If she was going to grow out of her condition, it would have happened by now. She's getting worse, not better. I feel so sorry for her. Imagine not being able to speak at your own birthday party!"

"I know it's a long shot," Dad says, "but maybe this new

woman will have some answers about Sunny's condition. She seems pretty sensible and she's got to be more use than Doctor Hogan." Dad gives a sniff. I don't think he likes Doctor Hogan very much. "Have you told Sunny about her yet?"

*No*, I think, *she hasn't*. I bet "this new woman" is a new therapist. I pull a face as Mum says, "Not yet, but I will. Oh, Smiles, do you think she'll be able to help Sunny? What kind of life will she have if she can't speak to anyone? She'll never go to college or have a boyfriend or anything like that, or even get a job. It's so unfair. I just want her to be happy."

"I know, Nadia. Me too."

"I feel so helpless." Mum starts crying and Dad holds her tight. I know he is upset too, though, and cross. He always wants to fix everything, to be in control. But there are some things that he can't fix. Like me. Mum's really upset and it's all my fault.

"Let's see how things go with this new specialist, love," Dad says when Mum's stopped crying. "But we may have to accept that Sunny's life will always be a bit different. And it could be worse – at least she's healthy. She has good friends in Mollie and Alanna, and she and Min adore each other. Would a quiet life on the island be so bad?"

"I suppose not," Mum says, her voice still a bit hiccupy from crying. "I'm sorry. It's just I love her so much. I want her to go to college, see the world, be happy..."

Dad strokes her hair. "I know you do, love. Me too. More than anything. But we need to take things day by day and try not to stress about the future. Once upon a time we thought we'd never have a family. And now we're blessed with two beautiful daughters."

"You're right." Mum wipes away the last of her tears. "We are lucky. I'm being silly. Do you remember the first time we saw them? Min was tiny and she was holding Sunny's hand so tightly I thought she'd break it. Neither of them had a word of English."

"And their faces when they saw the castle for the first time and realized this was their home!" Dad said.

"I wish we'd filmed it. They looked so surprised and so happy. It made my heart sing. Our own little family." Mum smiles.

"Let's not talk about this any more. Not tonight. I think I can hear—"

At that very moment Min bursts through the kitchen door, with Goldie trotting behind her. "Is dinner ready?" she asks. "I'm starving."

"Min Sullivan, don't be so rude," Dad says. "Come here to me, Minnie Mouse." As Mum turns away to dab her face with a tea towel – not that Min has noticed her wet cheeks or red eyes – Dad picks Min up and throws her in the air.

I shift the rug back over the crack in the floor, then creep over to the window seat and flop down, my thoughts racing. I wish I didn't put my parents through so much.

# Chapter 5

On Saturday morning, we're sitting at the table having our breakfast when Goldie pads into the kitchen with a dead mouse in his mouth.

"Yuck, Goldie," Min says. "Dad, he's got a mouse again."

Mum gives an ear-splitting shriek and jumps onto the table, waving her hands in front of her face. "Get it out of here!" she screams. "Now!"

Dad laughs. "It's dead, Nadia. It's not going to hurt you."

"You know I hate those things," Mum says. "I'm not coming down until it's outside and Goldie's been washed."

"You're being ridiculous, Nadia," Dad says, but he drags Goldie out by the collar. After a few minutes, once Mum's absolutely sure Goldie's outside and being cleaned with the hose, she climbs off the table and sits down. But she lifts her feet off the floor and tucks them under her bum.

"What's a mouse phobia called, Mum?" Min asks.

"I don't know – why?"

"No reason." Min gives me a knowing look. "Does Dad have a phobia?" she asks. While she's talking, I power up my laptop, which was at the far end of the table.

"No," Mum says. "Although he thinks raisins are the devil's food. He won't eat anything with raisins in. And he hates cooked mushrooms and anything slimy. But they're not phobias exactly."

"I have arach—" Min breaks off and looks at me. "What's it called again, Sunny?"

"Arachnophobia. And Mum's is musophobia," I say, reading off my computer screen.

"Everyone's scared of something," Mum says. I know she's thinking about me and my "phobia". But she doesn't mention it. I actually did a search for that one too – glossophobia – fear of speaking.

"We have a visitor coming on Monday, Sunny," she says, breaking into my thoughts. "Rosie Lee. She's a speech therapist."

I pull a face. So that's the "new woman" they were talking about the other night. I wondered when they'd get round to telling me about her.

"I've talked to Rosie on the phone and she sounds really nice," Mum says brightly. "I hope you'll give her a chance."

I try to say "Yes", but I can't. Just thinking about this stranger makes my throat go tight. So I nod instead. I'm ridiculous. Sunny Sullivan, the thirteen-year-old nodding freak.

On Monday morning, after she's walked Min to school with Goldie, Mum comes home with Rosie Lee. Mum and I talked about Rosie's visit more last night. Mum said she would be coming over on the morning ferry and would spend the day with us. I peer through one of the long arrow-slit windows in the living room and watch as Mum opens the front door and steps back to allow the woman in.

Rosie Lee doesn't look like the other doctors and psychologists I've met. She's younger, for a start, and she's wearing a long stripy scarf that looks like she knitted it herself, with a denim jacket and red jeans. Most of my other doctors have worn suits. She has curly blonde hair down to her shoulders. I only have a few moments before Mum will call me down to meet her, so I back away from the window and take some deep breaths until I hear Mum's footsteps on the stairs.

"Sunny," she says, coming into the room, "Rosie is here. She's in the kitchen. I thought we could make some fairy cakes together. Would you like that?"

I shrug. I'm too nervous to speak. But Mum understands. "Rosie's worked with lots of children with your condition," she says.

"She won't think I'm weird, like Doctor Hogan does?" I whisper.

Mum colours a little. "Doctor Hogan never said that."

"He said what I have is really rare."

"Well, it might seem rare to Doctor Hogan, but Rosie's different. This is her special area, and she really wants to help you."

"OK. I'll come and meet her."

I follow Mum silently down the stairs and into the kitchen. My heart is pounding and my palms are sticky. Rosie is sitting at the kitchen table and she smiles at me. I stare down at the floor.

"You must be Sunny," she says. "I'm Rosie."

"Would you like some tea, Rosie?" Mum asks. "Or coffee? And then I thought we'd make some fairy cakes together. Sunny's great at baking. She helps in the kitchen at the Songbird Cafe."

"I'd love a cup of tea, please," Rosie says. "And fairy cakes sound delicious. Is that the cafe down by the harbour? It looks lovely." She has a nice voice, low and calm.

"That's right," Mum says. "Sunny, while I'm making the tea, Rosie's going to talk to you for a few minutes. Maybe you could sit next to her?"

I nod and lift my gaze. Rosie is smiling at me. She has a really open, friendly face, with freckles across her nose. After taking a few deep breaths, I sit down beside her.

"There's absolutely no pressure to speak today, Sunny," Rosie says. "Your mum and dad have explained that you only talk to them and your sister. And only at home or where you feel safe, like in the car or a private room, is that right?"

I nod again.

"I'm a speech therapist," she continues. "And you're not to worry. It won't be like this for ever – I promise. I've helped lots of children just like you who find speaking hard. Your parents said starting school on the island was difficult for you and that was when your problem first began. I'm not surprised. Schools are very different to home. And you hadn't been speaking English very long, so that must have made it even harder. You were probably scared and worried about getting things mixed up. Is that right?"

I nod firmly. I found English really difficult at first and everything about school terrified me. On my first day, I was so worried about being separated from Mum and Dad and Min that I was shaking like a leaf. I was too scared to even ask to go to the toilet – I just couldn't get the words out – so I wet myself. Lauren Cotter called me "Soggy Pants" from that moment on. She bullied me so badly, but I didn't tell anyone except Min what was happening. And she told Mum. After that, Mum took me out of school and taught me herself.

Rosie leans towards me. "You try to speak, don't you? But you get scared and your voice gets all caught up in your throat. Something's stopping your voice coming out, isn't it?" She touches her hand to her throat.

That's it exactly! She really does get it. I nod again.

"Most people don't understand, but I do," she adds. "You know what your condition's called, don't you, Sunny? Selective mutism. It is unusual, but there are seven girls or boys just like you in every thousand. So you're not alone."

I give her a small smile. It makes me feel better knowing that it's not just me.

Rosie smiles back. "That's enough talking for the moment. Let's make these famous fairy cakes your mum promised.

We're going to spend this morning getting to know each other a little better. I have some art books to show you once we've finished baking. You like art, don't you?"

I give another nod.

"She's brilliant at drawing," Mum says, sliding a steaming mug of tea in front of Rosie and then sitting down at the table with her own.

"Thanks for the tea, Nadia." Rosie smiles over at Mum. "And don't worry, Sunny. Like now, I'll be doing all the talking and your mum will stay in the room. And then after lunch we'll do one final thing before I go down to the ferry – an exercise called sliding in. I'll tell you more about it later. Is that OK?"

I nod again. I like the way she's explaining everything to me. Knowing what to expect makes me less nervous. Goldie pads into the room then and Rosie reaches down and rubs him behind his ears – the way he likes it.

"Beautiful dog," Rosie says. "You must love him, Sunny. What's his name, Nadia?"

"Goldie," Mum says. "And, yes, she's mad about him. Sunny adores dogs. She had one in China called Puggy."

I'm surprised that Mum remembers Puggy. I told her about him a long time ago. Puggy was small and black. When I sat at the table to draw, he would jump onto my knees and curl up, like a live hot-water bottle. His yap was high-pitched, almost squeaky. Papa hated it – "mouse-bark" he used to call it – but I thought it was very sweet. When Papa died, we had to give Puggy to our neighbour Mama Wei.

"We're off to China in two weeks, in fact," Mum says. "The trip is Sunny's birthday present. She just turned thirteen."

"Happy birthday, Sunny," Rosie says. She looks at me for a moment. "China? It's quite a long trip, isn't it? How do you feel about that?"

I shrug and stare down at the table. Right now I'm more nervous about Rosie and what she might expect of me today. I reach down and stroke Goldie's silky head.

"You're very brave to go, Sunny," Rosie says. "I'm sure it'll be brilliant. I've always wanted to visit China. Will you show me the photos when you get back?"

I nod, my fingers resting on Goldie's warm back.

"Would it be OK if Goldie stayed with us today?" Rosie asks Mum.

"Of course," Mum replies. "I think Sunny would like that."

Rosie takes a sip of her tea and then looks around the kitchen. "Amazing place you have here. Did you do it up yourselves?"

"Yes," Mum says proudly. "Or rather, the architect and the builders did. Me and Smiles, sorry, John, my husband, were very involved, though. He's on a conference call this morning, but he's going to join us for lunch. We worked in Hong Kong for years, and when we came back, we wanted to live somewhere quiet with lots of space. We fell head over heels with this place when we first saw it. It's a complete money pit, but we love it."

"I can see why. What do your girls make of living in a castle? Must be pretty exciting?"

Mum smiles. "They love it. Sunny's sketchbooks are full of drawings of the castle and the island."

"I can't wait to see her sketchbooks." Rosie turns to me. "If you don't mind showing them to me, Sunny?"

I shrug, then give a nod.

"I'd love Sunny to go to art college some day," Mum says. "There's an art course on Sherkin Island, so she wouldn't have to travel too far if she didn't want to."

Rosie looks at me. "That probably sounds like a scary thought right now, Sunny. Art college, I mean. But anything's possible. Let's just take it one step at a time. Don't worry about the future for the moment."

I nod at her gratefully. Right now, even leaving the house can be scary. I can't imagine going to college. It's like telling me that I'll climb Mount Everest one day. Mum and Dad have all these big hopes for me. I don't want them to be disappointed.

Once Rosie and Mum have finished their tea, we start making the fairy cakes. Well, Rosie and I do. Mum just takes out the ingredients and the equipment and then watches.

I check the quantities in my recipe book. Then I weigh the butter and sugar on our pink kitchen scales and put them in a bowl. I love weighing things – it's fun! Alanna always lets me do that bit in the cafe. After that, Rosie creams the butter and sugar together in a big bowl, while I carefully crack the eggs into a smaller bowl.

"I can tell you've done that before," Rosie says. "I always get egg white all over the counter or shell in the bowl."

I smile at her as I beat the whites and yolks together. Then I point at the larger bowl.

"Yes," she says, understanding my gesture, "you add the egg and I'll stir." When it's all mixed in, Rosie asks, "Do you mind if I lick the spoon?"

Mum laughs. I'd almost forgotten she was in the room.

"Min loves doing that too," Mum says. "Go ahead. I'm sure Sunny won't mind."

I shake my head and smile again. Then I weigh the final ingredient – the flour. Once that's folded in, I spoon a dollop of the mixture into each of the cake cases that Mum has laid out on two trays. When each one is half full, Mum pops the trays into the oven.

"I can't wait to eat them," Rosie says. "How long will they take?"

I read the recipe book, then hold up both my hands and then only one hand.

"Fifteen minutes," Rosie says. "Perfect."

"Would you like to see the rest of the castle while we're waiting?" Mum asks.

Rosie grins. "I was hoping you'd say that."

# Chapter 6

Rosie loves our castle. She says it's like something out of a fairy tale. As we show her around, she "ooh"s and "ahh"s. She gets especially excited when we walk up the wooden stairs towards the parapets.

"Can you actually go outside onto the roof?" she asks.

"Yes," Mum says. "The edge of it anyway. Wait till you see the view."

There's a small landing at the top of the stairs. On it is a suit of armour that Dad bought. I used to think it was rusty, until Dad explained it was made from copper. It's so windy outside that the suit rattles when Mum opens the door onto the thin walkway that runs around the top of the castle.

"I think your soldier's about to come alive," Rosie says.

"That suit of armour is John's pride and joy," Mum says. "It's from Cromwell's time. John loves history. He collects old coins and lead shot from muskets. We found loads of both when they were rebuilding this place. Ready to go out?"

Rosie beams. "You bet."

"Watch your step," Mum says as she leads her outside.

I follow behind them and watch as Rosie shakes her head at the view.

"Just look at that!" she says. She has to talk loudly over the wind, which is whipping her hair around her face. "Is that Fastnet Lighthouse?"

"Yes," Mum says. "Amazing, isn't it?"

It's cold up here, so we only stay outside for a few minutes. Rosie's eyes are watering from the icy wind by the time we get back inside, and she hugs herself and rubs her upper arms. "This is the most incredible house ever. Thanks for showing me around, girls."

After the tour of the house, Mum and Rosie go back down to the kitchen to collect Rosie's things. I wait for them in the sitting room with Goldie. My sketchbook and pencil are on the coffee table, so I pick them up and start to draw more of my latest comic strip. It's about a fairy called Lotus Flower who is looking for her sister, Cherry Blossom, in a strange land – a crowded city of the future, full of towering glass skyscrapers, sky cars and robots. Lotus Flower's quest is almost impossible as she can only talk to her own kind – other fairies – not humans or robots, and Lotus Flower and Cherry Blossom are the only fairies left in the whole world. Luckily, Lotus Flower has Firecracker, her tiny talking dog, to help her.

As I hear footsteps coming up the stairs, my stomach starts to go jittery again. I'm worried that Rosie will expect me to speak, despite what she said earlier. I put down my pencil and do some milkshake breathing.

When Mum and Rosie come into the living room, I'm giving Goldie a rub. There's a tray in Mum's hands. On it is a pitcher of her homemade lemonade, three glasses, three side plates and a large plate piled high with golden fairy cakes. "I'll put this down on the coffee table so everyone can help themselves and I'll sit over there." Mum gestures with her head at the armchair. "And, Rosie, you take a seat next to Sunny on the sofa."

As soon as Mum puts down the tray, the delicious smell of the cakes wafts towards me. But I'm so anxious, I know I won't be able to swallow one.

Rosie sees me looking at the cakes and hesitating. "Would you like to have a snack later?" she asks. "I'm sure your mum won't mind."

I nod at her gratefully.

"Good idea," Mum says. When she moves the tray onto the side table, I'm relieved.

"I'll read my book now," Mum tells Rosie. "If you need anything, just ask." She takes a crime novel out of her back pocket, sits down and opens it.

"Thanks, Nadia. Right, Sunny, I have something special in here to show you." Rosie unzips her red rucksack and pulls out a large spiral-bound sketchpad, plus a pencil case, which is full of really cool Derwent art pencils, all different leads – soft and hard – a plastic bag of oil pastels and a whole rainbow of Sharpies.

"As I said before," Rosie goes on, "there's no need to talk unless you'd like to, Sunny. If you have anything you want to share with me, you can write it down or draw something if you'd prefer." She opens the sketchpad and taps a blank page. "And your mum is staying here, remember?" she adds. "And Goldie too."

I give Rosie another nod. I feel much more relaxed now.

She smiles back at me. "Good. Now, I want to show you some of my favourite paintings and drawings. Then maybe you can show me which ones you like." She takes a white hardback book out of her rucksack. It says "Art" on the front cover in red letters. There are coloured sticky notes marking lots of the pages. Rosie thumbs through the book.

"There," she says, opening to a page with a painting of a woman with black hair, dark eyes, red lips and eyebrows that meet in the middle. She's not pretty exactly, but she's strangely beautiful. I can't take my eyes off her. There's a small black monkey on her left shoulder and a dog in front of her.

"Frida Kahlo," Rosie says. "It's a self-portrait. I love the way she's staring straight out of the picture, like she's challenging you. She looks like she's thinking deeply about something, doesn't she?"

Rosie turns the page and there she is again – Frida Kahlo. This time she's painted herself with green jungle leaves behind her. There's a monkey, a cat and a bird in the picture too – but what really catches my eye is the necklace made of thorns around her neck. Some of the thorns are piercing her skin.

I stare at the picture for a long time, taking in what I'm seeing.

"Her art really makes you think, doesn't it?" Rosie says. "That's why I like it. She had a hard life. When she was a teenager she had a terrible accident and was in pain for most of her life. She had to paint lying down sometimes." She shows me a photo of Frida lying on her back, painting in bed. "Would you like to see another painting I love?"

I nod.

She flicks back through the pages until she comes to a swirling blue night sky. The stars are picked out in bright yellow.

"'The Starry Night' by Vincent van Gogh," Rosie says. "I love the colours. And also in this picture, by Monet." She turns to another painting. This time it's one I recognize – a pond with pink, blue and green water lilies.

"We saw some Monet paintings in Paris last year," Mum says, looking up from her book. "Sunny loved the art galleries."

"I'm sure she did." Rosie smiles at me again. "This one makes me feel calm and happy. I can imagine myself floating over the lilies in a rowing boat, the sun on my face. The last painting I'm going to show you is the 'Mona Lisa'. I bet you know it too."

I nod. Everyone knows the "Mona Lisa" and her strange half-smile.

"Do you think she looks happy or sad, Sunny?" Rosie asks.

"Bored," I write on the sketchpad. "From sitting still for the artist."

Rosie laughs. "You're probably right. I prefer the Frida Kahlo portraits myself. They're full of emotion, aren't they?"

I nod again.

"The best paintings make you think, don't they? And they make you feel something. Lots of artists express their feelings through their art. How do *you* feel, Sunny? When you think about speaking in front of strangers, I mean. Can you draw it for me?"

She's been so kind to me, showing me all the paintings and talking to me like a real person, that I take a pencil out of her pencil case – a 4B, which has a nice soft lead – and start to draw.

I imagine that I have to speak to Rosie, right now. My heart starts to beat faster and I get that familiar scared and jittery feeling, like I have no control over my body or anything that's happening to me.

I draw a girl in a dark forest. The trees are reaching for her, their branches pressing into her skin, like the thorns in the Frida Kahlo painting, until she's crushed. She's alone and scared. There is no one to come and save her. Using an even softer 8B pencil, I frame the forest with a black box. Then I fill the box with swirling shapes, pushing the tip of the pencil into the paper, harder, harder, until suddenly the lead snaps. I drop my head, feeling ashamed that I've ruined Rosie's pencil.

"Don't worry, Sunny; the pencils are there to be used," Rosie says. "And that's an amazing picture. Is that you lost in the forest? With all those trees attacking you?"

I shrug, looking down at the floor, still feeling bad about her pencil.

"Sunny, do you feel you are under a lot of pressure to talk and be a 'normal' girl?"

I nod.

"I hear you, Sunny," she says. "I hear you."

And even though I haven't said a word, I know Rosie's telling the truth.

# Chapter 7

Before lunch, I draw more pictures for Rosie. I use my own
sketchbook – hers reminds me of the forest. Rosie's very
interested in China, so I sketch her some pictures of my life
there: the apartment, the park we used to play in with the red
wooden humpback bridge over the pond, and Puggy. Dogs are
hard to draw, but I do my best.

"He looks like a right little scamp," Rosie says of Puggy
with a laugh.

I smile and nod. He was always stealing Mama's silk
slippers and chewing them so the stuffing came out.

Mum is looking at the drawings with interest. "What's that
in the park?" she asks. "The piece of stone?"

"Chessboard," I write on the sketchpad.

"Ah, right, of course. I'd forgotten about the outdoor chess
games," Mum says. "Where we lived it was mainly old men
playing. They sometimes brought their birds with them in
beautiful cages. Did you ever see them, Sunny?"

I nod enthusiastically. The man who lived next door to us
in Shenzhen walked his bird every morning. It was tiny and

blue and sang the most beautiful song. I used to bump into him on the way to school with Mama and then, after she died, with Mama Wei. I draw a quick sketch of him and his bird's ornate cage.

"Is that someone you knew, Sunny?" Mum asks.

I write, "Our neighbour in Shenzhen," underneath the drawing.

"Anyone hungry?" Dad asks, coming into the room, rubbing his stomach. "I certainly am. The bagels are heating in the oven so you'd better be quick." He smiles at Rosie. "You must be Miss Lee. Nadia's told me all about you. I'm John, Sunny's dad. But everyone calls me Smiles. We're hoping you can work miracles with our girl here."

Rosie stands up and shakes his hand. "Rosie, please. And I don't know about miracles, but I'll certainly do my best. That's one fine artist you have there. And a very smart girl."

"We think so," Dad says. His eyes are gleaming. I can tell he's pleased and that makes me happy. All I've ever wanted to do is make my parents proud of me.

During lunch, Dad asks Rosie how we are getting on.

"Very well, thanks," she says. "Sunny is great company."

Dad looks surprised at that. I guess he's not used to people describing me as "great company".

"We were looking at an art book this morning and she has excellent taste," Rosie adds.

"She's got a good eye, all right," Dad says. "So what's the plan for this afternoon? Something a bit more scientific, I hope."

"Smiles!" Mum glares at him.

Dad puts his hands in the air. "Ignore me. It's just…" He breaks off and sighs. "I really want this to work, that's all. Sunny means the world to us."

"I understand, Smiles," Rosie says. "But these things take time. You can't expect immediate results. And pressure is the last thing Sunny needs right now. She has to feel supported and accepted. You need to trust me. I know what I'm doing."

"You're right," Dad says. "I'm sorry. I was out of line. You're the expert. And I do trust you. And, Sunny, I don't mean to put pressure on you. We just want you to be happy."

I press my hand on his to say, *I know, Dad.*

"And since you were asking, we'll be playing Monopoly this afternoon, Smiles," Rosie says. "But there is a scientific reason for it, I promise." She grins at him, her eyes twinkling. I'm starting to like Rosie more and more.

Once lunch is cleared away, Dad goes back to work and Rosie goes upstairs to fetch her rucksack.

"Everything all right, Sunny?" Mum asks when Rosie's left the kitchen.

I listen for Rosie, but I can't hear her. She must still be upstairs. "Yes," I say, my voice mouse-like.

"You're doing great." Mum gives me a hug. "I'm really proud of you. Rosie's nice, isn't she?"

I hear Rosie's footsteps in the corridor so I just nod.

When Rosie comes back into the room, she tells me that we are going to try something called "sliding in". "You're going to play Monopoly with your mum and I'm going to sit outside in the hallway," she explains. "Then in five minutes I will come back in, but I want you to keep talking to your mum as if I'm not there. I'll only stay one minute and I won't say anything. Do you think you can do that, Sunny?"

The hot worried feeling swamps my body again. I can't do that. I want to, but it scares me too much.

"Sunny?" Rosie asks gently. "Can we try?"

I shake my head furiously.

"OK then." She doesn't sound cross, thank goodness. "How about if I stay outside the room with the door closed to start with? Can you show me how far away I need to be for you to feel comfortable talking normally?"

"Will you go outside the door and show Rosie, pet?" Mum asks me. I can tell from the intense concerned look on her face that she really wants me to try this. I give a tiny nod and lead Rosie out of the room. Mum comes with us.

"How about here?" Rosie asks, pointing halfway down the corridor.

I shake my head and point at the chair further down the hall, right by the front door.

"Will you use your normal voice if I sit there?" Rosie asks. "Not a whisper. The kitchen door will be closed."

I think about this for a second. If the door is closed, then, yes, I think I can do that.

I nod.

Rosie smiles. "Good for you, Sunny. That's a very positive start."

With Rosie outside in the hall, Mum and I set up the Monopoly board on the kitchen table. It's Mum's game from years ago and the box is faded and battered, but I love playing it even more because of that.

"What do you want to be?" she asks, picking up some of the small metal playing pieces and showing them to me. "Car, top hat or dog?"

I take a deep breath. "Dog," I manage to say, surprising myself. My voice is low, but it's more than a whisper. I did it! I said something, even though Rosie is just outside. She can't possibly hear my voice – all the wooden doors in the castle are centimetres thick – but it's still a huge thing for me.

Mum must think so too because her eyes have gone suspiciously glittery and she blinks a few times before she says, "I'll be the car. And the bank." When we play as a family, she's always the bank. Min can't be trusted with the money, I find doing the bank too much like maths and Dad says it reminds him of work.

We start playing Monopoly together, just like a normal mother and daughter. When I land on Dawson Street, my favourite property, Mum asks me if I want to buy it.

And I say, "Yes, definitely!" really loudly, which makes her smile so widely I think her mouth is going to crack.

"I thought you'd say that," she says.

I'm about to ask to buy another property when I hear a noise outside the door.

A second later, Rosie walks in. "How are you getting on, Sunny?"

I shrug.

"She owns half of Dublin at this stage." Mum waves at the Monopoly board. "She always wins."

"And you were OK talking when I was in the hall?" Rosie asks me.

I nod.

Rosie smiles. "Good for you. Now I'm going to ask you to do something incredibly brave, Sunny. When I leave the room this time, I'm going to leave the door open a tiny crack, but I want you to continue talking as normal."

With the door open, she'll be able to hear my voice. I can't do it – I just can't.

"I know this is stressful for you," Rosie says. "But I'd really like you to try. Take a couple of deep breaths. Remember the art we were looking at this morning? Think of Monet's lily pond – all green and peaceful. Shut your eyes and see if you can visualize yourself floating on that pond in a little rowing boat. Can you do that for me?"

I breathe deeply and close my eyes. Then I imagine that I'm lying back in a boat and Min's rowing me through the calm green water. When I open my eyes again, Rosie has left the room. The door is a tiny bit open, and I can't take my eyes off it.

"Sunny?" Mum says. "It's your turn to throw."

I concentrate on the board again. I throw a six and a four and move my dog ten places, landing on Kildare Street.

"Do you want to buy it?" Mum asks. She looks at me hopefully. I know she's willing me to speak.

I open my mouth, but nothing comes out. I close it and nod. I can tell she's disappointed, but she's trying not to show it.

We play for a while longer, until I have houses on all my pink properties. Every time Mum lands on one of them, she has to pay me lots of rent.

When she lands on Dawson Street, I let out a cheer and punch the air. "Yay!" I say.

Mum looks at me in astonishment. Her hand jumps to her mouth. "Sunny," she says. "Oh, Sunny." Then I remember – Rosie. She can hear me. I instantly go silent, but inside I'm happy and a little shocked. I said something in front of a stranger! OK, so it was only a cheer – barely even a word – and it only happened because I'd forgotten Rosie was there, but I did it.

Mum gives me a huge smile. "You've nearly bankrupted me. Will we finish the game?"

I draw my finger across my throat, to say, *You're dead, Mum.* She just smiles.

When we've finished the game, Mum calls Rosie back into the room.

"From the grin on your face, Sunny, I'd say you were the clear winner," Rosie says. "And was that you cheering? I heard a lovely happy sound at one stage. Good for you. That's a huge achievement. Today has been really successful. We've reached two targets: you speaking while I was in the hall with the door closed *and* with the door open. You should be very proud of yourself. It's been quite an intense day and I'm sure you're tired. Thank you for all your hard work."

"Thank *you*, Rosie," Mum says. "We appreciate it, don't we, Sunny?"

I nod. A wave of exhaustion hits me and I yawn, setting Mum and Rosie off.

Rosie laughs. "Yawns certainly are contagious."

Rosie has to catch the four o'clock ferry back to the mainland. Mum goes with her to collect Min, who has been doing her homework at Alanna's cafe after school. As soon as she gets back, Min comes into my room, uninvited, and starts bouncing up and down on my bed.

"Who was that lady in the funny scarf with Mum?" she asks. "Your new doctor?"

"Speech therapist, actually," I tell her from my desk. I'm on my laptop, looking up some of the artists Rosie showed me earlier. "She's called Rosie. She came just after you left for school."

"Why was she here so long?" Min asks. "What did you do all day?"

"We baked fairy cakes and looked at art and played Monopoly."

Min stares at me. "That's so unfair. I had to do a maths test today and it was horrible. But guess what Harry Lannigan did at lunch?"

Just then Mum sticks her head around the door. "Min, leave your sister alone. You have homework to finish. We'll talk over dinner."

Min rolls her eyes. "Fine." She huffs out of the room.

"So what else did you do with the Rosie lady?" Min asks as soon as we sit down for dinner. She's like Goldie with a bone – she never gives up. "Play Connect Four?"

I shrug.

"You're as bad as your father, Min," Mum says for me. "All the activities had a purpose. Sunny has made wonderful progress already. She even spoke in front of Rosie."

Min's mouth falls open "Really? A whole sentence, you mean, in front of a stranger? *Finally!*"

"Don't be unkind," Mum says. "And, no, it wasn't a sentence. It was a word – but it's still a big breakthrough."

"Rosie was sitting in the hall while your mum and Sunny played Monopoly and they left the door open," Dad explains. "Sunny shrieked or cried out or something when Mum landed on one of her properties. And Rosie heard her." His voice sounds a bit flat. I get the feeling that he's not as impressed by my "breakthrough" as Mum is.

"Sunny said 'Yay'," Mum says proudly.

"*Yay?*" Min pulls a face. "Is that it? It's not even a word."

"Try to be more supportive of your sister, please, Min," Mum says.

"OK, that's great, Sunny," Min says quickly. "Well done. Now, can we talk about my day? It was so funny at lunch because Harry Lannigan got this piece of popcorn—"

"Min, we were talking about your sister. Please don't interrupt. And try to be a bit more patient, Smiles. Rosie's coming back to work with Sunny after we get home from China. She's hoping—"

She's cut off by a pea flying out of Min's left nostril and across the table. The pea bounces off Dad's chest and lands on the floor. Goldie jumps out from under the table and eats it off the tiles.

"Yuck!" I say. "That was up Min's nose, Goldie."

"Min, go to your room," Mum says. "Right now."

"But I was just showing you what Harry Lannigan did with his popcorn today," Min says. "No one ever listens to me."

"That was disgusting, Min," Mum says. "You do not put food up your nose and snort it out like that. Ever. It's dangerous and revolting. Leave the table, please. Now!"

After jumping up from her chair, Min marches past us all, her face like thunder. As she passes by my chair, she mutters, "Stupid Sunny."

She's such a delightful sister sometimes.

# Chapter 8

Min's been in a funny mood all week. She's had several arguments with Mum over silly things, like yesterday morning when she tried to go to school in shorts with bare legs, until Mum stopped her and made her put woolly tights on underneath. Then earlier today she refused to take Goldie out because she said it was my turn. It turned out she was right, but Mum wasn't happy about how stroppy she got about it Thankfully, she seems to have snapped out of it by the afternoon. She comes home from school in a much better humour.

"Can I go down to the cafe when I've finished my homework?" she asks Mum, dumping her school bag on the kitchen table. "Sunny, you can come too if you want. It's nearly May Day and Alanna wants us to help her make some decorations."

"Oh, Mum, can we go?" I ask. "Please?" It would be nice to see Alanna, and I love May Day. Alanna always holds a special celebration at the Songbird, with a May Bush and everything!

The first time Alanna told me and Min about the May

Bush – which is actually a small tree covered in decorations – I thought she was joking.

"It's to ward off fairy mischief," she said. "The fairies move from their winter residence to their summer palace on May Day and it's always best to keep them happy when they're marching. They like looking at pretty, shiny things so we leave coins for them under the tree, as well as cakes and buns. Most fairies have a sweet tooth."

Min put her hands on her hips. "Fairies? Are you teasing us, Alanna? Fairies don't exist!"

Alanna lowered her voice as she said, "Don't let any of the older islanders hear you, Min. They all believe fairies are real. People believe in a lot of things that can't be explained, like angels and gods, so why not fairies?" I looked at Alanna in surprise. I wanted to ask whether anyone on the island had actually seen a fairy, but of course I couldn't. Having no voice is so frustrating.

"What about you, Alanna?" Min asked. "Do you believe in them?"

"I certainly do," she said.

"Then I believe in them as well," Min said and I nodded. We've been firm believers ever since.

It's a dull grey day and the Songbird Cafe is quiet. Alanna is behind the counter when we arrive. As we walk towards her, she looks up and smiles. "Excellent timing, girls. Have you ever blown eggs?"

"Is that some sort of weird game?" Min asks. "Like the egg-and-spoon race?"

Alanna laughs. "No! We're going to use painted eggshells to decorate our May Bush this year. So, ready to blow some eggs?"

"Yes!" Min says excitedly, as she dashes through the kitchen door. Before I can follow her, Alanna puts her hand on my arm.

"I've seen some of your drawings of the Little People, Sunny," she says. "They're amazing. Can you do a small one for the May Bush? I'll roll it up and tie it with a ribbon like a little scroll. The fairies love special gifts."

I nod at her shyly. Alanna is one of the few people who has seen my drawings, and I'm proud she thinks my work is good.

I cover the pages of my sketchbooks with lots of things – the castle, Click, Goldie – but my favourite things to draw are fairies, or the Little People, as Alanna calls them. Not pink Disney fairies with fluffy wings, but proper fairies in floaty dresses, with pointy ears, long limbs and big eyes. And my fairies come from all over the world. My Lotus Flower and Cherry Blossom fairies are Chinese, for instance, like me and Min. All my fairies are gentle and kind, but they are also clever and sometimes mischievous, because that's how I imagine them. I've never actually seen one, of course. But maybe I will one day.

"I'm waiting!" Min calls from the kitchen.

When we walk inside, Min is tapping her foot impatiently. "How do we do this egg thingy then?" she asks.

"With this." Alanna picks up a large needle. She selects an egg, washes it and then carefully pricks holes in the top and the bottom of the shell, one a little bigger than the other. She holds the egg over a glass mixing bowl and gently blows into the smaller hole. The gooey centre starts to run into the bowl through the larger hole.

"It's magic," Min says, clapping her hands together. "Can I have a go?"

Alanna smiles. "Of course. We have dozens to do. I'm sure you'll be very good at it, Min. You're full of hot air."

"Hey!" Min looks offended.

I grin at Alanna and she grins back.

After Min and I have blown twenty eggs between us – and it's a lot harder than Alanna made it look; Min breaks at least half of hers – Alanna comes back into the kitchen to check on us.

"How's it going, girls?" she asks.

"OK," Min says. "But can we do something else now? My cheeks are sore from all the huffing and puffing. I feel like the wolf in *The Three Little Pigs*."

Alanna laughs. "Sure. They need to be decorated now anyway. You can paint what you like on them – butterflies, dragons or just a zigzag pattern. How about using a nice bright red paint like on those Chinese lanterns we made for Sunny's birthday? That reminds me – your trip's really soon. Are you excited? Do you remember much about China, Sunny?"

I shrug. I wish I could tell Alanna how nervous I am about

going back to China. I think she'd understand. I'd also like to explain that even though I love Mum and Dad, I miss Mama and Papa. Little Bird is my home, but sometimes I still feel like an outsider here. I can't talk to Mum and Dad about any of this because I don't want to upset them, and I don't think Min would understand – she's too young.

I begin to feel claustrophobic in the small kitchen. I need some air, so I point to the door and Alanna nods. "It's hot in here, all right, and you look a little flushed. Min, you stay here and decorate the eggs. I'm going to get some fresh air with Sunny."

"But I need help with the eggs!" Min says.

"I know, but your sister needs me too."

"She always comes first," Min mutters.

"I'll be back to help you in a few minutes, Min," Alanna says. "I promise."

Once outside, I take a couple of deep breaths and gaze towards the sea, trying to calm myself down.

The closer the trip to China gets, the more anxious I feel. I'm worried about all those strangers, about getting lost, but most of all about bringing back sad memories of my Chinese family and everything that happened in the orphanage.

Alanna stands beside me, staring out into the bay. "It's all right to be nervous about the trip. But, remember, you're a lot stronger than you think." She takes my hand and holds it tight. "You'll find your way. I know you will. And I'm here if you ever want to—" She breaks off abruptly. She was about to say "talk".

"If you ever need a friend," she says instead. "Remember that. You can count on me, little nightingale."

I squeeze her hand.

"I'm sure your parents will understand if you really don't want to go," she adds.

I smile at her to say, *Thanks*. But I can't cancel the trip. Mum and Dad wouldn't be angry, although Min would kill me. For days I've heard nothing but China this and China that from my sister. How Chinese people invented money, clocks, fireworks, kites... But the real reason I can't cancel the trip is this: I keep hoping that visiting my past home will stop me worrying so much and make me able to speak. How it will do this, I don't know. But what I do know is that I don't want to be silent Sunny for ever.

# Chapter 9

"I'm not sure about all this May Day nonsense tomorrow," Mum says, drumming her fingers on the kitchen table. The four of us are having breakfast together. "It'll be dark at that hour of the morning. What if something happens to you? I know Alanna says it's an island tradition the year you turn thirteen, but you're only eight, Min."

"Nearly nine," Min says. "And Sunny can't go without me. For obvious reasons." She mimes not being able to talk. "And we're only washing our faces in dew and collecting slugs. What's going to happen to us? Ooh, attack of the deadly Little Bird slugs. *Doo-do doo-do*," Min sings in a spooky voice, wiggling her fingers in the air.

I giggle – Min can be quite funny sometimes. Dad puts his hand over his mouth and I can tell he's trying not to laugh too.

"Don't encourage her," Mum tells me with a frown. Uh-oh, I think Mum's in one of her sensitive moods. She does look tired. She hasn't bothered with make-up today and the skin around her eyes is dark.

"We have to be in the field before sunrise for the dew thing to work," I say. "And Alanna will look after us. We'll be fine, Mum. Please?"

Mum murmurs something under her breath. Mum likes Alanna, but she thinks most of Alanna's traditional spells and herbal remedies are nonsense. "A load of old hocus pocus," she always says.

Dad puts his hand over Mum's. "Sunny's right, love, they'll be grand. It's a bit of fun – let them go."

Mum sighs. "I hate it when you all gang up on me. And don't come running home when you slip on all that dew and break your ankles, girls."

"We won't be running anywhere if we break our ankles," Min says.

"Doh!" Dad joins in.

Mum's had enough. After glaring at Dad, she stands up and walks out of the room. She gets upset easily and she doesn't like being teased – who does?

I look at Dad. "Shouldn't you go after her?"

"Don't worry about your mum," he says. "She just has a few things on her mind."

"So can we go out with Alanna or not?" Min asks, ignoring what just happened.

"I guess so," Dad says. "But if you wake us up at four in the morning, I swear I'll murder the both of you. Leave the house quietly. And don't be bringing any blooming slugs back with you either, got it?" He shudders. Dad hates slugs and snails as much as he hates slimy food.

"Got it, Pops," Min says. "Thanks. You're the best." She gives him a big hug. He chuckles, delighted, and ruffles her hair. I wish I could throw my arms around him like that. If only I could worry less and be more fun. If only my life was easy, like Min's.

I've never been outside at four in the morning before, and it's exciting, but a bit creepy. Alanna offered to come and collect us from the castle, but Min wanted to walk down to the harbour, just the two of us. She said it would be more of an adventure that way. Mum wasn't keen, but Dad talked her round. Goldie wanted to tag along, but we decided it was better to leave him in the kitchen as he might bark and wake people up – not that there are many people on Little Bird to disturb.

As we're walking down the lane towards the harbour, where we're meeting Alanna and Mollie, I have to keep breaking into a run to keep up with Min, who is hyper-keen to get there. Min insisted on carrying the torch and she's swinging it around, so it's hard for me to see the road properly. The moon is still casting a ghostly glow over everything.

"This is going to be so much fun," Min says. "I can't believe Mum let us out."

"It'll be fun until you spot a rat or something."

"I like rats," Min says firmly, trying to sound all brave.

"How can you like rats? They're disgusting. They eat rubbish."

"I just do."

65

There's never any point in arguing with Min – she never changes her mind – so I say nothing. Also, we're drawing close to the harbour and I can see Alanna and Mollie waiting for us under the lamp, which means they might be able to hear me. Mollie's in a silver-and-black striped sweatshirt and Alanna's wearing her big red cloak with the hood that makes her look like Little Red Riding Hood. I smile to myself. One of the things I love about Alanna is that she never worries about what other people think – she just wears what she likes. And, boy, does she have some strange clothes.

Min sprints the last few feet towards them, taking the torch with her and leaving me to stumble the rest of the way in the dark.

"OK, where's this magic dew you've been promising us?" she's asking Alanna when I join them. "Will it really make my skin beautiful?"

Alanna smiles. "Good morning to you too, Min. Hi, Sunny. And, yes, it's certainly supposed to. Follow me, girls. We'll try the grass beside Red Moll's Castle. I'll explain what to do when we get there. And then I'll show you some special May Day fortune-telling."

"Hey, Sunny." Mollie bumps her shoulder gently against mine. "You OK?"

I smile at her.

"Don't know about you, but I'm half asleep," she continues. "You awake?"

I shrug and then nod.

We follow Alanna up the hill and climb over the gate that leads into the field surrounding the castle ruins. The grass is glistening with tiny drops of water and I'm glad that Mum made us wear our wellies.

"Now, soak these cloths in the dew, girls," Alanna says. She hands us each a square of white muslin the size of a face cloth. "And then dab them on your skin and you'll all have beautiful complexions for the whole year."

"Here's hoping." Mollie bends down and rests the cloth on the grass for a few seconds. Then she pats the damp square over her face. "It's actually very refreshing. A bit cold, though. Hope it sorts out my spots. I hate them."

"Everyone gets spots. It's perfectly normal," Alanna says. "You have lovely skin, Mollie."

"Thanks," Mollie says happily and she dabs the cloth over her face again.

We all do the same, soaking our cloths and bathing our faces. Mollie's right – it's nice: cool and tingly.

As she washes her face, Min wiggles her bum and sings a song that she's made up to the tune of "Call Me Maybe": "I've just met dew, And this is crazy, But feel my skin, It's gorgeous, maybe." She bursts into giggles at the end.

"Min!" Mollie groans. "That's terrible." But we're all grinning at her antics. My little sister may be crazy, but she is funny.

# Chapter 10

That afternoon we go to Alanna's cafe to meet Landy. According to Mollie, he's found something in the woods behind Lough Cara that he's desperate to show us because we're the only people on the island who will appreciate it. He refused to tell her what it was, though, and we're all dying to know, especially Min. Alanna has to stay and run the cafe, so Mollie promised to fill her in when we get back.

It only takes about fifteen minutes to walk from the cafe to the woods, but we have to go past the edge of Lough Cara and it's always tricky to avoid the swarms of midges that hover near the water. Sometimes the tourists wade in the rushes on the banks and disturb them, and, boy, do they regret it!

"Come on, Landy," Min moans as we tramp around the lake. "What's the big secret? What are we looking for? Is it a squirrel or something? I love squirrels."

"I'm not saying, Min, so stop asking," he says.

She pulls a face at him.

"She's been up since four this morning," Mollie says. "She might be a bit tired."

"I'm not tired!" Min looks disgusted.

"What were you doing up at four?" Landy asks.

"We were bathing our faces in dew and making May Day spells with Alanna," Min explains. Then she makes her voice go all mysterious. "We were discovering the name of our one true love."

"Really?" Landy says. "Go on, tell me. Who's your one true love, Min?"

"The name begins with an L," she says, gazing at him like a lovesick puppy. She's shameless! Landy just grins, though. He knows all about Min's crush on him and thinks it's funny.

Mollie snorts with laughter. "Min, it was so not an L. It was more like a W."

"It could have been an L," Min says stubbornly. "Maybe I just left my slug on the flour for too long."

"Slug?" Landy asks.

"We collected slugs and put them on a plate of flour," Min explains. "And they wrote the first letter of our true love's name in the flour with their slime."

Landy shakes his head. "You guys are bonkers. What about you and Sunny, Mollie? What letters did you get?"

"Sunny's was a C and my slug was too lazy to move," Mollie says.

"I'm glad you all like fortune-telling and magic," Landy says. "I knew you guys were the right people for this trip."

"Is that a clue?" Mollie asks.

"Might be," he says. "This way."

We follow him over the stone stile, into the trees, and then along the winding forest path. The air smells musty, of rotting leaves and damp moss. On one side of us is the lake, and on the other is the Atlantic Ocean. It's amazing to think that the next piece of land is America. Cara Woods is not a place any of us go very often. During the summer and at weekends, it's full of tourists hiking, but today we're completely alone.

Landy stops suddenly in front of a gnarly old oak tree, and points at its base.

"There," he says and steps back so that we can all see.

I peer at the tree trunk and then I spot it – a small wooden door, pointed at the top like a church door. Its doorstep is covered in coins and tiny metal trinkets, like the ones on my charm bracelet.

Min gasps. "What is it?"

"The door to a fairy house," Landy says.

Her eyes widen. "Have you tried opening it?"

He shakes his head. "No. You try, Min."

Min crouches down and pulls gently on the miniscule metal door handle. "Doesn't work."

"Maybe you need a secret password that only the fairies know," Landy suggests.

Min's eyes light up. "I bet you're right. *Salla kazoom!*" she says, waving her hands in the air like a magician. Then she attempts to open the door again, but nothing happens, which is hardly surprising – *salla kazoom* is not exactly the most inspired fairy password.

"It's an amazing door, isn't it, Sunny?" Mollie says.

I nod.

"When did you find it?" she asks Landy.

"I spotted it the other day when I was down here with Dad cutting up fallen trees for firewood. It's not the only door I've found either. I've counted three so far and there may be more hidden deeper in the woods."

Mollie stares down at the door again. "Who made them, do you think? It wasn't you or your dad, was it?"

Landy laughs. "I wish. Whoever made that door is a woodwork genius."

"I thought you said it was the fairies," Min says, sounding cross. She must have believed what Landy told us. But if Min had read anything at all about the Little People, she would know that they keep themselves well hidden. They'd never let humans see their doorways.

"Maybe it is, Min," Landy says. "I'm not ruling it out."

"Really?" Mollie asks, surprised.

He shrugs. "There must be something behind all those old fairy myths. And look at all the coins and things that people have left on the doorstep. They're gifts for the fairies. To grant wishes. In fact, we should all make a wish right now and leave an offering. Here you go." Landy reaches into his pocket and then hands each of us a coin.

"Thanks, Landy," Min says, her eyes twinkling at him. She really does have it bad.

Mollie and Min place their coins on the doorstep.

I hold mine tightly in my hand.

"Sunny?" Mollie says. "Aren't you going to make a wish?"

What's the point? If the Little People do exist, they know what I want. It's what I've wanted for years – to be able to speak.

*I'm sorry, fairies,* I think as I place my coin on the pile. *I'm happy to give you this coin, but right now I'm all wished out.*

"Can we see the other fairy houses now?" Min asks, hopping from foot to foot.

Mollie rolls her eyes at me and I smile. Min's so impatient, but I'm glad to see she's back to her usual self. I was beginning to wonder what I'd done to annoy her.

We find the second one easily – a midnight-blue door set into the earth under a big twisted tree root. The third one is harder to spot.

"I think it's down by the lake," Landy says. After leaving the path and climbing over some fallen tree trunks, we reach the mud and rushes at the edge of Lough Cara.

"There it is," Landy says, pointing at a rocky outcrop. This one isn't just a door but a whole house! It is made from wood and painted a mossy green, and is three storeys tall. It has two small red chimneys sticking out of a real tile roof and Gothic windows with pointed tips. It's tucked under an overhanging rock to keep it dry.

"Someone's put a lot of work into that," Mollie says, crouching down to look at it more closely.

I look around then, wondering why Min isn't squealing

with excitement. She loves this kind of thing. I can't see her anywhere. Where is she?

Mollie and Landy are so busy studying the house and talking about the real glass in the windows that they haven't noticed she's missing. I peer into the forest, looking for her yellow rain jacket or pink wellies, but I can't see anything.

I pull at Mollie's sleeve. "Beautiful, isn't it?" she says, gesturing at the house.

"Min," I mouth at her.

"Sorry, Sunny? I don't understand."

I mouth my sister's name again, but she's still not getting it, so I tweak her arm and then point at the forest behind us.

"You're right, Sunny. Min will love this one," Landy says, standing up.

I shake my head and wave my arms around while mouthing "Min" again. This time, Mollie clicks.

"Oh, Min!" she cries. "Where is she?"

I throw both my hands up to say, *I don't know*.

"Min!" Mollie calls loudly.

Landy joins in. "Min!" he shouts. "Can you hear us?"

There's a splash from further down the lake. My heart stops. Min is a terrible swimmer. If she's fallen in...

Then there's a shout. "Over here! Help! I think I'm stuck."

It's Min.

Relief floods over me and I run towards the sound of her voice. She's at the edge of the lake, up to her knees in sinking mud. When I reach her, she pulls one leg out, but the boot

73

stays behind. *Stay still,* I want to tell her, *you're going to lose your balance otherwise.* And just as I think it, Min tips sideways and lands in the brown gloop.

"Min!" Mollie yells, coming up behind me. "What are you doing? You'll sink in that mud. It's dangerous. Get up."

Min is lying on her side in the soft mud, squealing. The mud is up to the top of her legs and she's sinking fast.

"I thought I'd be able to get out on my own," she says. "Stupid mud." She hits the mud with her hand, making a big splash.

"Stay still, Min, or you'll sink even deeper," Landy says. "I'm coming in to get you."

"I'll help you," Mollie tells him.

He wades in slowly, and it takes a while, but he finally manages to pull Min out by the arms. Mollie holds his waist to make sure he doesn't get sucked in too. Then, while Landy lifts Min onto solid ground, Mollie tries to fish out Min's boots with a stick. It's no use – they're stuck in too far.

"You shouldn't go near that lake mud, Min," Landy says when they're all back beside me on dry land. "It's lethal stuff. Every year at least one cow or sheep gets stuck in it. And they're not as lucky as you. They don't always get rescued. Sometimes they drown."

I shiver. Min may drive me crazy, but I don't want to lose her.

"What were you doing in the mud anyway?" Mollie asks.

"Looking for another fairy house," Min says huffily. "Landy

said there might be more hidden around the place."

"In the forest," Mollie says. "Not in the mud. Come and see the one we found and then we'd better get you home before you freeze to death."

"I have no boots," Min says. "Someone's going to have to carry me." She looks pointedly at Landy.

Mollie rolls her eyes at me, but Landy just laughs.

"No problem, Min," he says. "I'll get you home safely."

I'm so relieved that Min is all right that I don't even feel irritated. That's my sister for you. She can wrap anyone around her little finger.

After taking another quick look at the fairy house, we walk back home with Min riding high on Landy's shoulders, her filthy jeans matting his blond hair with mud.

I love her so much. Despite how much she annoys me sometimes, she means everything to me. And I couldn't even tell my friends that she was in danger. As the reality of it all sinks in, I realize that I have to get better, for my sister's sake as much as my own. How can I possibly keep her safe otherwise?

# Chapter 11

On the afternoon we're leaving for China, Mum's in a complete flap. She's racing around the house, collecting even more of our clothes to squeeze into an already bulging suitcase. Dad and Min are waiting in the jeep outside. They've just dropped Goldie off at Mollie's house. Dad is getting impatient now. He keeps beeping the horn, which is making Mum even more frazzled.

"Mum, they're waiting for us," I tell her as she stuffs raincoats into our suitcase, along with more swimming costumes.

"I thought it was supposed to be hot," I add. "And I've already packed my togs. I don't need another pair."

Dad beeps the horn again.

"OK, OK," Mum mutters. "I'm coming." She shuts the final suitcase and I wheel it outside while she locks up the house.

Dad gets out of the jeep to load up the boot. "Do you have the passports?" he asks her.

Mum looks anxious for a moment, then rummages in her handbag, pulls out her pink leather travel wallet and opens it.

"All here. Plus the tickets and the visas." She tucks everything safely back into her bag.

"And I have plenty of Hong Kong dollars, Chinese yuan and my credit cards." Dad gives her a hug. "Stop worrying, Nadia. If we've forgotten anything, we can buy it over there."

It takes nearly two hours to get to Cork airport and then it's another two hours before we arrive at Heathrow in London, where we will catch the plane to Hong Kong.

The boarding area at Heathrow is brightly lit, with a lot of glass and steel. And it's so busy! There are people everywhere, bustling along with wheelie suitcases, dozing on the seats, or hunched over playing games on their iPads, or reading.

I spot a Chinese family with a daughter who looks just like Min, although she's a bit younger, I think – six or seven. I catch the girl glancing at me and Min and then at Mum and Dad. In Ireland, it is me and Min that people stare at because we're the ones who look different, so it's funny for Mum and Dad to be examined so closely. To this Chinese girl we must look like a strange family unit, with our two pale-skinned Irish parents. I wonder if she has worked out that we're adopted.

No one else in my family has noticed the girl. They're not as observant as me. Being quiet and slipping into the background has its advantages.

Min's moaning breaks into my thoughts. We haven't even got on the plane for Hong Kong yet and she's already complaining loudly. Unlike me, she's not afraid of making a scene. She's lying with her head on Mum's lap and sighing every few seconds.

"This is really boring," she moans. "When will they let us on the plane?"

Mum strokes her head. "Soon, pet," she says. "You're just tired. It's way past your bedtime. Hopefully you'll sleep during the flight."

Min sits up. "Are you crazy? I'm much too excited to sleep. I can't wait to see all the skyscrapers and the lights. What's the first thing we're going to do when we get to Hong Kong?"

"Rest after all the travelling," Mum says.

Min fakes a yawn. "Boring. No, I mean, the first fun thing?"

"As soon as we've checked into the hotel, we're going to take you to our favourite noodle bar in Hong Kong," Dad says. "Lucky's. Then we'll visit the city on the mainland, Kowloon, and The Peak on Hong Kong Island. The Peak is where we used to live. It's really pretty around there. The hotel we're staying in is near the harbour, but it's not far from our old apartment. Then we'll do lots more sightseeing and finally, on our last day, we might visit Shenzhen and the orphanage – but that's Sunny's choice."

"What about me?" Min asks. "How come she gets a choice about what we're doing and I don't? It's not fair."

"This is Sunny's birthday trip, Min," Mum says. "You'll get your own trip another time."

"It better be a good one," Min says.

Mum frowns at her. "Min Sullivan, stop being such a madam. Why don't you play your DS until we board?"

While Min is busy with her new Pokémon game, I pull my sketchbook out of my rucksack, open to a fresh page and start drawing Puggy. Since meeting Rosie, I've been sketching him quite a lot and I've got much better at capturing his funny sticky-out left ear and his paws. I use the side of my pencil lead to shade in his soft velvety fur. I begin to add a cherry tree beside him, but then I stop and rub it out. No! I don't want to remember anything about the orphanage. Instead, I draw our old home, remembering the musty smell in the lift of the tower block and its flickering light. And the cats. Lots of silky grey cats. They didn't live in our block, though. I can't recall exactly where I saw them or who owned them, but I have a feeling that they weren't strays.

And then I sketch our funny old neighbour Mama Wei, with her wrinkly brown face like a walnut. When Mama died, Mama Wei looked after Min during the day and collected me from school when Papa was working in the factory. She was strict but kind and she cooked great noodles. She used to let Puggy stay with us in the afternoons. She understood that having Puggy around to hug and curl up with helped me to deal with how much I missed Mama (Min was too small to remember Mama). Puggy loved snuggling.

"Are you sure we're supposed to be in this bit?" Min whispers, after the air steward has shown us to our seats in business class. "We're not posh business people. We're just kids."

"Anyone who can pay for the seats is welcome in business class," Dad says. "Trust me."

"It's a lovely treat, isn't it, girls?" Mum says. "I for one am looking forward to lying down. I know we only left the island this afternoon, but it feels like we've been travelling for days." She yawns, making me yawn too.

The seats are really cool, much bigger than normal ones on aeroplanes. They fold down into mini-beds too, and they have their own built-in movie screens. The air steward brings us chicken and noodles to eat with a choice of real metal cutlery or chopsticks. We all choose chopsticks. Then Mum makes us put on our pyjamas and do our teeth in the tiny loo.

Min falls asleep almost as soon as she lies down. So much for being too excited to rest! Dad's been snoring away since the minute they dimmed the lights – he never has any problem sleeping – and Mum has just dozed off too. So it's only me still awake. I'm lying here with my eyes closed, trying to get to sleep, but my mind won't let me. Behind me, the Chinese girl from the boarding area is being settled down.

"Close your eyes now, little one," her mum is telling her in Cantonese.

"Can I have a song, Mama?" the girl asks.

Her mum starts to sing very softly, a song about a little bird:

*"Once I saw a little bird come hop, hop hop.*
*And I cried, 'Little bird, please stop, stop, stop…'"*

I know that song! Mama used to sing it to me and Min every night. I close my eyes and try to imagine that it's Mama singing to me.

Mama.

I have a photo of her tucked into the back of my sketch-book. In it she is about ten years old. She's wearing a traditional red-and-blue silk tunic dress over matching trousers. She is small like Min, with paintbrush plaits and bright eyes. I also have a photo of Puggy – his coat all shiny and black. And a photo of Mama and Papa's wedding day. Papa's in a smart black suit and Mama's wearing a red silk dress with a gold dragon twisting down the front. Her hair's tied up in a bun and there's a red flower tucked behind her ear. She looks beautiful.

The final photograph that I have is of my whole Chinese family: Mama, Papa, me and Min. It was taken just after Min was born and she is all wrapped up like a caterpillar in a white blanket. Mama is holding her tight against her chest. Papa is next to Mama, his bald head shining in the light, just like his eyes. I am standing in front of them both, looking a bit serious, and Papa has his hand on my shoulder.

Mum and Dad don't know I have these photos and I've never shown them to Min. They're the only thing I still have from my old life and I want to keep them a secret, just for me – my own special link to China. Usually they live in a shoebox at the bottom of my wardrobe with my other special things, but I put them in the back of my sketchbook before we left the house this afternoon because I wanted to bring them with me.

I check that Mum is fast asleep and then I slide out the wedding photo and study it. Mama smiles at me with dark laughing eyes. Papa's smiling too. He's holding Mama's hand, his chin tilted up proudly. I hold the photo in my hand, drinking them in, before slipping it away again.

Finally I drift off to sleep, Mama's bird nursery rhyme running through my head and my sketchbook still firmly clutched in my hands.

# Chapter 12

China! We're finally in China. I feel a rush of excitement as I wait to step off the plane. Mum is standing beside me. Dad and Min are in front of us. Min asked the air steward if she could be the first person off the plane, because she'd been born in China and this was the first time she'd been back. I was mortified and Mum seemed a bit embarrassed too, but Dad thought it was hilarious. The air steward said he'd make sure of it. He asked me if I wanted to join Min, but I shook my head and stared down at the floor.

"She never talks," Min said. "It's really boring."

Mum told the man that we'd follow on behind. When he'd gone, she gave out to Min for being mean to me, but my darling little sister went all huffy. "I was just telling the truth," she said.

She was, but it still hurt.

There's a crowd of people behind us now, all anxiously waiting for the doors of the plane to open so they can disembark. I can feel their impatience bubbling and snapping at our heels. It's making me nervous.

Mum leans towards me. "Special day for you, pet. For all of

us. First Sullivan family visit to China – the country that gave us our two beautiful daughters."

I nod.

She presses her lips together, the way she always does when she's trying not to cry. The last time she was in China was when she collected me and Min from the orphanage. I guess being back here reminds her of all that. I take her hand and squeeze it to say, *I know, Mum*.

"Thanks, Sunny," she says. "You're my best girl – you know that, don't you? I love you so much." Tears spring to her eyes.

I give her a *Mum, come on!* look and she smiles again and wipes her tears away with her fingertips.

"Sorry. Just your old mum getting emotional. Ignore me, sweetheart."

The plane's door is wide open now and the air steward waves Min goodbye and wishes her a good trip.

"Ready, Sunny?" Mum asks me.

I nod. My heart is racing, so I take a few deep breaths. As I walk out onto the plane's steps, a wave of hot air hits me. It smells different to Irish air – metallic, sharp and strangely familiar. I squeeze Mum's hand again.

"Warm, isn't it?" she says. "Not like rainy old Cork, eh?"

Then we make our way down the steps and onto Chinese soil.

We walk up towards the airport building. Min and Dad are about ten strides ahead, Min dragging Dad along by the arm. She's so impatient. I wish she'd wait for us. I always thought we'd share this moment together. Then suddenly she turns around and gives me a big smile and I start to feel better.

Once we're in the main building, I stop and look out of the window. The sky is bright yet hazy, like there's a thin grey veil over the sun.

"That's the smog," Mum says, reading my mind. "Do you remember it?"

I nod. There's a surge of bodies behind us, pressing us forwards, and Mum says, "Better keep moving, Sunny. Let's try to catch up with your dad and Min. Now, do I have the passports or does he have them?" She drops my hand and starts searching in her bag.

I continue walking, gazing out at the tower blocks in the near distance, thinking how strangely familiar everything is starting to feel. The hazy sun, the buildings, the smell, even the smog. And the number of people. In my memories of China, there are always hundreds and hundreds of people, all bustling along.

The next thing I know, I've lost Mum. She was just beside me, but now she's disappeared. I climb onto some orange plastic seats near by so I can study the crowd ahead of me. When I still can't see her, I start to panic. I have to find her!

A Chinese woman about Mum's age comes up and asks me if I'm all right. I just stare at her, helplessly. Even the thought of speaking to her makes me more scared. After a while, the woman shrugs and moves on.

I'm afraid I'm going to faint, so I step off the seat and sit down on it instead. What if I can't find Mum or Dad? I don't even know the name of the hotel we're staying in. Tears fill my eyes and I wipe them away.

I look up when I hear someone else say, "Are you all right?" in Cantonese. An official-looking man in a white short-sleeved shirt is standing in front of me.

I shake my head.

"Are you lost?" he asks.

I nod.

"What is your name? You cannot stay there," he says when I don't answer. "Do you understand? Please follow me."

I stay glued to my seat, terrified.

"You must come with me to the office," he says, irritated. "You cannot sit here on your own." He reaches down to take my arm, but I shift away from him. I'm finding it hard to catch my breath, so I have to gasp in little puffs of air and my chest is starting to sting, like someone's squeezing it really hard. I know this is just a panic attack, because I've had them before, but it still feels horrible and scary.

"Sunny? Oh, thank God." It's Mum.

"Do you know this girl?" the man asks, this time in English.

"Yes," Mum says. "She's my daughter. Thanks for your help."

The man is looking at me curiously. "Is she all right? Does she need medical assistance?"

"No, she'll be fine in a minute," Mum says. "She's just

having an anxiety attack. We're good, thank you."

Mum sits down beside me as the man walks away. My chest is still incredibly tight and I'm gasping for air. "You're going to be OK, Sunny. You just got a fright. Try to take deep breaths." I feel Mum's hand on my back. "Remember your milkshake breathing. Big breath in, and blow it out, nice and slow. Try to follow my voice. In … out. In … out. That's it, good girl. Keep going. In … out…"

I do as she says, and slowly my breath goes back to normal and the pain in my chest starts to disappear. After a few minutes, I lift my head and look at Mum. I've never been so happy to see her in all my life.

"What happened?" she asks. "You were just gone. I'm so sorry I lost you, pet."

My eyes well up again.

"Oh, Sunny." Mum starts crying too. "You must have been so scared. Especially when that man came over and you couldn't talk to him."

"There you are." Dad appears through the crowd, with Min riding on his shoulders. "We were wondering where you'd both got to."

"I lost Sunny for a moment, Smiles," Mum says. "She was right beside me and the next minute she'd disappeared. It gave me such a shock."

"Nadia! How could you…?" Dad stops talking when he sees how upset Mum is. Instead he smiles gently at me.

"We're all together now, that's the main thing," he says.

"Hong Kong's a very busy place, girls. From now on we're not going to let you out of our sight. And if you do get lost, stay exactly where you are and ask someone who looks official for help."

"Sunny can't do that, Dad," Min says.

"Sorry, of course," Dad says. "We'll give you a piece of paper with our mobile numbers on it, Sunny, and instructions asking the person who finds you to ring us immediately. We'll write it in English and Cantonese and Mandarin. Cover all bases."

I know he means well, but that makes me feel so small. Away from Little Bird and everything I know, I'm as helpless as a baby.

# Chapter 13

"I love this hotel," Min says, bouncing on the super-king-sized mattress of Mum and Dad's bed while I look out of the window. "What's it called again?"

Dad frowns at her. "The Four Seasons. And you're going to break that bed, Min."

Min stops jumping and flops down belly first on the puffy feather duvet, which gives a gentle sigh underneath her. Mum's taking a shower in the huge cream marble bathroom before we head out together for our first dinner in China.

"I want to *live* in this hotel," Min says. "For ever and ever. And eat room service and swim in the pools every day." The hotel has *two* swimming pools – at two different temperatures.

Dad walks over to stand beside me. "Quite a view, all right. That's Kowloon over there on the mainland." He points to the ultra-modern-looking skyscrapers across the water. "We're on Hong Kong Island now, but we'll go over to Kowloon tomorrow. Right now, I'm starving. Let's go and wait for your mum downstairs." Min's so full of beans I think he's worried she'll wreck the room if he doesn't get her outside.

* * *

"Small girl with the black hair and the cherry T-shirt," Dad whispers to Min as we sit in the lobby.

Min studies the girl for a second then says, "Cherry Red. Dedicated to keeping little kids safe from robbers and kidnappers."

"What's her super power?" Dad asks.

"Poison. Each of those innocent-looking cherries on her T-shirt is actually a deadly poison-loaded bomb. She can pluck them off and throw them at baddies, killing them instantly."

"No killing in the superhero game," Dad reminds her.

"Freezing them instantly then," Min says. "My turn. Tall man in the suit holding a briefcase. With the glasses."

"Tricky one." Dad sucks in his breath. "How about Super Glasses Man? Those are no ordinary glasses. They can see through, um…" Dad's struggling a bit. "Clothes."

Min tilts her head. "To look for guns and things? Or to see ladies' boobies?"

"Min!" Dad looks appalled, but then his expression breaks and he starts to laugh. "No! To look for guns and explosives."

Min fakes a yawn. "Boring. That's a rubbish superhero. What do you think, Sunny? Who wins?"

I point at Min.

"Yeah!" She jumps off the sofa and does a little wiggling-bum victory dance.

"Thanks, Sunny," Dad says grumpily. "She only won

because I'm jet-lagged." He's ultra-competitive and a bad loser. He takes every game seriously, even silly ones like this. Mum says that's what makes him so good at his job – he's an oil trader – so we shouldn't tease him about it.

"Let's play again," Min says. "Me first this time. Boy in the stripy top with the headphones." Min points at a good-looking Chinese boy of about fourteen who is nodding his head to his music.

"Supersonic Ear Boy," Mum says, sneaking up on us and making me jump. "His hearing is so sensitive that he has to wear those earphones to deaden sound. Oh, and he can even make out thoughts. So he can hear Sunny thinking he's cute."

I thump her on the arm.

Mum just laughs. "So, everyone ready? I've been waiting for you guys for ages. What kept you?"

"Ha, ha, Mother," Min says. "Very funny. Race you all to the door."

As she tears away, Dad shouts after her, "Min Sullivan, what did we tell you about running off?"

Min is waiting for us outside the entrance to the hotel. It's the early evening now, but the air outside is still warm and smoggy. It catches at the back of your throat like builder's dust.

"Next time, you wait inside the door, young lady," Dad says sternly. "I mean it. This isn't Ireland, Min – understand?"

"OK, sorry," Min says, the smile dropping off her face.

"We wouldn't want to lose you, pet, that's all," Mum says.

"Remember what happened to Sunny at the airport?"

"It wouldn't happen to me," Min says. "I'm not an idiot who won't speak to people."

"I've warned you before about being unkind to your sister," Mum says. "You know it's not Sunny's fault."

Min rolls her eyes. "It's always about Sunny. Sunny, Sunny, Sunny."

"Min, that's enough!" Mum snaps.

"It's OK, Nadia," Dad says, putting his hand on Mum's arm. "I think Min gets it. And you won't do it again, will you, Min? Say sorry to Sunny."

"Sorry," Min mutters, but I can tell she doesn't mean it.

"Ready to do a little exploring before dinner, girls?" Dad says.

"Yes! And hurry up, slowcoaches, there's a taxi." Min waves her arms in the air and a yellow cab pulls up in front of the entrance.

"Let me or your mum do that, please, Min," says Dad.

We all bundle into the taxi – Dad in the front, and me, Min and Mum in the back. On the way to the restaurant, Mum talks to the driver in Cantonese.

"My daughters, Soon Yi and Min Yen," she says.

The driver tells Mum that we are beautiful girls.

"*Dohjeh,*" Mum says. Thank you.

I mouth the word to myself, hearing Mama's voice ringing in my ears. It was one of the first words she ever taught me. "Don't forget your pleases and thank yous, Soon Yi," she always said. "It shows respect to your elders." There are different words that mean thank you in Cantonese. *Dohjeh* is for when someone gives you a gift or a compliment, *mhgoi* is for when someone helps you.

"Mum, when did you first learn Cantonese?" Min asks. "When you were my age?"

Mum laughs. "No, a long time after that. I was a teacher here, remember? I had lots of Chinese students and I did some evening classes. My Cantonese came in very useful when we were adopting you, because your Chinese family spoke it too. That's pretty unusual. Lots of people in Shenzhen speak Mandarin instead. The adoption agency was surprised – but pleased, I think – that I was able to speak to you both in your native language."

I'll never forget Mum speaking in Cantonese the first time we met her. It made me feel less afraid and less alone. She said, "Hello, Soon Yi and Min Yen. We're so happy to finally meet you."

"Well, I can speak *three* languages," Min says. "English, Irish and Cantonese."

I glare at Min. She knows a few words of Cantonese – Mum taught her – but she can't "speak" it, not the way I can. I wish I could show her, by talking to the driver. But even the thought of opening my mouth in front of him makes me feel sick.

"Tell us about our Collection Day," Min pipes up, oblivious to the fact that I'm staring at her.

"Let's save it until Monday," Dad says. "It's a long way to

Shenzhen, Min. We'll have plenty of time for stories on the drive."

I stare out of the window again. I vividly remember seeing my new white parents for the first time. I was terrified, literally shaking all over. But once I realized that the smiling couple really was taking both of us, me and Min, and that Mum knew Cantonese, I stopped being quite so scared.

"Sunny? Did you hear what I said?" Min says.

I shake my head. I wasn't listening.

"I was asking what kind of noodles you are going to order."

I just shrug.

"You're in a very weird mood, Sunny," she says. "I was born here too, you know. You're lucky – at least you remember Mama and Papa. I don't remember much. Stop being so mopey."

"Min!" Mum says. "Leave your sister alone. I'm not telling you again."

"I'm just saying…"

"Don't! Look out of the window."

"I'm bored of that." Min pouts.

"OK. Do you want to hear about the guinea pigs we kept at the school here?"

"Guinea pigs? Didn't they get a bit hot?"

As Mum starts to tell Min about the school she used to work in and their pet guinea pigs, I feel even more depressed. How come my sister is such a chatterbox and I'm like this? It's not fair!

I'm so frustrated I want to scream. To take my mind

off things, I gaze at the brightly lit shops, burger joints and restaurants, all carefully slotted together like building bricks.

The taxi driver pulls down a side road and then stops. While Dad's paying him, Min, who's sandwiched between me and Mum, climbs over me, and swings the taxi door open. She's about to jump out, but I grab her ponytail to stop her.

"Ouch!" she shrieks. "Mum, Sunny pulled my hair."

"Close the door this instant, Min," Mum says. "You never get out of a car on the traffic side. You could get run down. I do wish you'd use your head. Sunny was just trying to stop you killing yourself."

Min is still scowling at me. "But she hurt me." She's rubbing her head at the base of her ponytail and scowling.

"Next time, grab her arm instead, Sunny," Mum tells me. "Now stop the squealing, Min, and get out of the taxi on the other side this time."

I'm not sorry I pulled Min's hair, even though it was a genuine accident. She's been making digs at me since we left home and I'm sick of it. I know it's her trip too, but she has no idea how annoying it is not being able to communicate. And remembering how pretty Mama was and how kind Papa was makes everything worse. I love Mum and Dad so much, but it doesn't mean I don't think about my old life sometimes too. And being back here makes it all seem so real again.

After we get out of the car, Min shoves the door closed behind her with her bum. She may be tiny, but she's strong and it slams shut.

"I know you're tired," Mum says to her, "but I want you to behave."

"What did I do?" Min asks, all innocent.

"Come on, Min," Dad says, holding out his hand. "Let's go straight to the restaurant. Plenty of time for sightseeing tomorrow. I'm so ravenous I could eat a whole Minnie Mouse for dinner." He pretends to eat Min's arm and she squeals with delight.

"Let them walk on ahead, Sunny," Mum says, taking my hand. I wouldn't normally let her – I'm thirteen, after all – but we're on holiday. "I know she's picking on you, but she'll snap out of it soon. She just needs food."

I sigh and give a little nod to say, *I hope so*. We walk down the street together, passing lots of strange-looking shops. They spill out onto the street. Their large baskets – full of all kinds of orange, brown and grey dried food – litter the pavement. And, boy, do they smell! Like fish that's been left out in the sun too long. I recognize that scent. Then it comes to me. It's dried seafood: mussels, octopus tentacles and squid. Mama used to make soup with those ingredients.

*Suddenly, I'm four or five years old and walking down the street, holding Mama's hand tightly, the very same smell filling my nostrils. Mama stops outside a shop and starts chatting to one of the shopkeepers, while I pet his grey cats.*

The cats from my dreams! That's where I remember them from – a shop just like these. There were at least ten of them there, perched on shelves or stools or draped around each other in baskets, all purring away as I stroked their sleek fur. I smile to myself, happy memories of shopping with Mama flooding back to me: the feel of her warm palm in mine, her tinkling laugh as she joked with the shopkeepers, and the delicious little moon cakes she'd buy me if I'd been very good.

# Chapter 14

I roll over and look at the alarm clock beside my bed. Four in the morning. Last time I woke up it was three-thirty and I forced myself to go back to sleep. But now I'm wide awake. Min's still spark out. I can hear her snoring. The curtains are open a crack and there's just enough artificial light from outside to read by. I take my book from the bedside table, but I can't concentrate, so I put it down again. I wish it was seven o'clock. Mum and Dad said they didn't want to see Min until after seven and I promised I'd keep her entertained until then. But right now *I'm* the one that needs entertaining.

I climb out of bed as quietly as I can and creep towards my rucksack, which is on the floor beside the armchair. After pulling out my red sketchbook and a pencil, I curl up in the chair. I push the curtains open a little more with my foot and look out. There's an old-fashioned green ferry boat chugging across the harbour, so I start to draw it, and soon I'm lost in my picture.

After I've finished the ferry sketch, I do one of the skyscrapers across the bay in Kowloon and when I've completed that, I open a fresh page, and before I know what

I'm doing I'm sketching a large room filled with lots of metal cots, my hand moving faster and faster over the page. There are baby walkers neatly lined up against one wall and a row of metal sinks against another. Each cot holds a baby or toddler. In one, to the far left of the picture, I draw a toddler standing, her little hands reaching out. She's small. A wispy ponytail on the top of her head is tied with a bow.

"Is that me?" Min asks, surprising me.

I was so caught up in what I was doing I didn't notice her getting out of bed.

"The girl with the bow," she says. "That's me, right? In the orphanage?"

"Yes," I say. "You were cute back then."

"Hey! I'm cute now. Is that what it was like in the orphanage? Or are you making it up?"

"It's how I remember it. I guess we'll see how true it is when we visit."

She tilts her head. "Was the orphanage noisy? Sometimes I hear babies crying in my dreams."

I'm surprised. She's never mentioned anything about her dreams. "Yes, when new babies arrived, they cried a bit."

"What did Mama and Papa look like? Can you draw them for me?"

I think about showing her the photos, but I'm not ready to share them with anyone yet, not even Min. "Where is all this coming from, Min? You've never asked me much about them before."

"I know, but I guess being over here makes it all kind of real. The past stuff, I mean."

"I'll draw them for you one day," I say, "but not right now, OK? This is Puggy, though. Our dog." I flick back a few pages and show her my earlier drawing.

She runs her finger over the sketch, smudging it.

"Min!"

"Sorry."

I snap my sketchbook shut.

"Is that why you're being so weird?" she asks. "Because you keep remembering things? About when we were little?"

"I'm not being weird, Min – I'm just being quiet. Come on, you must be used to it." I don't want to talk about it right now. Besides, Min doesn't need to know how hard it was when Mama and then Papa died and we went to the orphanage, or about my constant worry that we would be separated.

"It's more than just your anxiety about talking in front of people," Min says. "Ever since we arrived, it's like you're on another planet."

"Min, you're *from* another planet." Then, to change the subject, I ask, "Are you up for having a Jacuzzi? Mum and Dad won't be up for ages."

"Can we put loads of bubbles in it?"

"Sure. As long as you don't make a mess."

"Me? Never."

I start to laugh.

* * *

Min is dancing around the bathroom completely naked and covered in foam when Mum bursts through the door. "Girls! What on earth is going on in here?" she says. "It's not even six."

"Oops," Min says.

I can't speak. I'm laughing too hard.

Mum tries to look cross, but the edges of her mouth are twitching. She starts to laugh. "What are you like? Get into the shower, both of you, and wash those bubbles off. There's foam everywhere."

"Dare you to get into the water with us," Min says, jumping back into the huge Jacuzzi. She poured so much bubble bath in that foam is spilling over the top. It's like one of those mad science experiments you see in the movies.

"Please?" Min begs. "You can wear your togs like Sunny."

Mum grins. "OK then."

We're having a full-blown foam fight by the time Dad comes in a few minutes later. Mum has slid under the water to avoid Min's latest attack, so Dad doesn't see her straight away.

"Girls!" Dad's voice is way louder than Mum's, especially when he's cross. "Stop that this instant. Your mum's going to kill you."

Mum resurfaces, rubbing bubbles off her face, and grins up at him. "Hi, Smiles."

He groans and shakes his head. "You're all insane. And you're the worst, Nadia. My three crazy Sullivan girls."

# Chapter 15

We're visiting Kowloon today. Tomorrow we're taking a tram to the top of The Peak – the highest part of Hong Kong Island – and on Friday, Saturday and Sunday we're doing more sightseeing here before going to Shenzhen and the orphanage on Monday. I'm trying not to think about that trip. I know it's going to bring back sad memories.

We've just had lunch (little Chinese dumplings called dim sum) and now we're walking up a wide, busy road called Nathan Street. Mum keeps veering off into shopping malls and I think Dad's getting a bit fed up.

"A toy shop. Can we go in?" Min squeals with excitement. She loves shopping as much as Mum does.

"Must we?" Dad complains. "I'm all shopped out."

"Just one more, Dad, please?" Min begs.

He allows her to pull him into the toy shop, and me and Mum follow them. Inside, it's small – the size of a caravan – and packed with shelves and shelves of Hello Kitty and Snoopy toys.

I spot a wall of cuddly monkeys. I pick one up – a fellow

the size of my hand, dressed in a tiger costume, complete with a hood and ears. He's adorable and I stroke his soft fur with my fingers. I've seen one just like it before. Then it comes to me in such a rush I almost gasp.

When Mama got very sick and had to stay in bed, I slipped my favourite toy – a monkey just like this one – under her sheet to look after her. I don't know what happened to it when she died, but I never got it back. Papa must have thrown it away.

Mum comes up behind me. "That's a Monchhichi. Sweet, isn't it? I had one when I was a child. Would you like it?"

I nod

I watch Mum talking to the shop assistant as she pays for everything – my one monkey and what looks like an entire Hello Kitty army for Min. Dad and Min are chatting to each other outside, and I feel very alone.


Up the road a bit, another familiar smell – this one exotic and sweet – is making my nose twitch. Where's it coming from? I stop dead in the middle of the street and look around.

"Sunny, what are you doing?" Dad asks, looking at me with concern.

I squeeze my nostrils to try to tell him about the smell. He just looks confused until Min says, "What is that?" She sniffs the air. "It's like sweets being burned on a bonfire."

Mum smiles. "Incense," she says. "They burn it in the Chinese temples. I think there's one down that side street, in fact. Would you like to find it, Sunny?"

"What about me?" Min says. "Maybe I'd like to see this temple thing as well."

"Yes, Min, you can come too," Mum says, her voice a bit weary. Min would wear anyone out.

We walk down the side street and then into a small open park. There are women sitting on benches under leafy trees, feeding the birds with scraps of bread, and old men standing around marble chessboards watching a game.

The smell is coming from the large building facing the park. It's amazing – like something out of a fairy tale, with its ruby-red pillars and tiered golden roof. Mama Wei used to take us to a temple just like this one to pray to her family gods. Min was only a toddler and I was allowed to push her pram.

"Would you like to go inside?" Mum asks me and I nod. Dad has wandered off to take some photographs.

"I want to come too!" Min says. "What is this place? It's cool. Is a temple like a palace, Mum?"

"It's a church," Mum says. "You can only come inside if you're quiet. Think you can manage that?"

"I'm brilliant at being quiet," Min says confidently.

I give Min a look and she sticks her tongue out at me. Inside the temple, the smoke from the incense is so strong it makes my eyes water.

"What are those?" Min points up at the smoking spirals hanging above our heads. They're like huge bed springs.

"Incense cones," Mum says. "Impressive, aren't they? They

must take days to burn. Watch out the ashes don't land on your head."

Mum leads us past the cones, towards the altar at the top of the building. "Those are gods," she says, nodding at the large statues that stand on the brightly decorated altar. "People leave offerings to them, like those oranges and apples, or coins and incense sticks. They do it to ask the gods to keep their family safe and sometimes to request special things like good exam results."

"Look, there are toys too," Min says, pointing at a small white teddy bear with a child's photo attached to its stomach with a rubber band. It's sitting next to a statue of a female god wearing a red robe and a gold crown. Her face looks kind. For the second time today my heart gives a jump. I recognize that statue. It's Mazu – the goddess of the sea, and one of the gods that Mama Wei prayed to.

I have an idea. After taking the toy shop bag out of Mum's hand, I reach inside and lift out the Monchhichi. Then I pull on Mum's sleeve and point at the altar.

Mum looks puzzled.

"I think she wants to leave the Monchhichi up there," Min says. "For the statue."

Mum seems taken aback. "Really?" she asks me.

I nod.

"Are you sure, Sunny?" Mum asks. "You've only just got it."

I nod again.

"I guess that's all right," Mum says, "if you really want to."

I really do. I carefully place my new Monchhichi beside

the white teddy. Then I close my eyes and say a prayer in my head.

*Dear Mazu, It's Soon Yi. I used to pray to you with Mama Wei. I'm trying to be a good sister and to look after Min, like I promised Mama. Anyway, I've left a present for you – it's a Monchhichi. I hope you like it.* I pause, then add, *I know it's a big thing to ask, but if you could help me with the whole speaking thing, that would be amazing. Thanks, Mazu.*

I open my eyes to find Min kneeling beside me, her eyes squeezed shut, her lips moving silently. I'm sure I see her mouth form the word "Sunny". Is Min saying a prayer for me too?

# Chapter 16

On Thursday morning we go up the side of a mountain in a rickety old tram. OK, The Peak is actually a hill, but it's a very big hill. Neither Mum nor I are fond of heights, so we don't enjoy it much. Min loves it, of course – anything dangerous or dramatic is right up her street. And Dad's lapping it up too, stretching out of his seat to take photos of the view.

When we reach the top, a huge zigzag of escalators whisks us up to the special viewing platform. The views are pretty spectacular – skyscrapers on one side, and the sea and a spooky-looking misty island on the other. Loads of the skyscrapers have swimming pools built halfway up them, so it looks like there are big patches of blue suspended in the air. I've never seen anything like it.

I stand at the wall and gaze over at the mainland, wondering whether it's possible to see Shenzhen from here.

Dad joins me. He must have read my mind because he says, "Shenzhen is over in that general direction." And he points across the bay, past Kowloon and slightly to the left. "Nervous about Monday, Sunny?"

I shrug. I am, but I don't want to worry him.

He squeezes my shoulder. "It's an amazing place, Hong Kong. We were very happy here, me and your mum. I'd forgotten how beautiful it is."

I want to tell him that Little Bird is beautiful too, and that I'm glad he and Mum brought us to Ireland – but I can't talk in public like this. So I stand on my toes and kiss him on the cheek instead.

We have a really nice lunch in a cafe called The Peak – burgers and chips for Dad and Min, Chinese noodles for me and Mum – and then we walk back down the hill to see where Mum and Dad used to live. Their apartment block is huge and built of stone the colour of coral. Me and Min count thirty-nine storeys. Mum says it has an underground gym and swimming pool, with a big hot tub.

"Can we live there?" Min asks.

"No way," Dad says. "I don't trust you girls and Jacuzzi bubbles one little bit."

We all laugh.

On Friday, Saturday and Sunday we do so much sightseeing that our feet nearly drop off. We visit a bird market, see a giant Buddha on an island and take a trip on the old-fashioned green Star Ferry that I spotted from our hotel bedroom window. On Sunday evening we're all so tired that Mum says we can order room service. After dinner, we flop down on Mum and Dad's giant bed. Even Min's exhausted, which is good as it means she's not yapping away or jumping on the bed.

"I don't know about you, girls, but I can barely keep my eyes open." Dad gives a huge yawn. "Early night for everyone. Big day tomorrow."

My stomach tightens. Tomorrow means Shenzhen and the orphanage.

"How long will it take to get there?" Mum asks.

"It's not far," Dad says, "only about fifty kilometres – but there will be a lot of traffic going through the city areas. The driver reckons it will take about two hours."

Mum looks at me. "It's not too late to change your mind about visiting, Sunny."

"I know," I say. But we've come so far and I'm aware that Mum and Dad want me to go. I can't let them down.

"How does it feel being back in China?" Dad asks. "It's been such a whirlwind we haven't really had a chance to talk about it yet. Is it how you remember it?"

"Kind of," I say. "But I don't remember ever being here on Hong Kong Island or in Kowloon. I remember temples and parks. And the food and the smelly seafood shops."

Mum smiles. "They'd be hard to forget, all right."

"I'd forgotten how busy it is, though," I add. "There are so many people."

"Does it scare you?" Mum asks. "The crowds, I mean."

I shrug. "I don't have to talk to the people in them so, no, not really." Here, everyone walks quickly, minding their own business. It's not like on Little Bird, where everyone wants to stop and chat all the time.

"What about you, Min?" Mum asks. "Does being here make you remember anything?"

"A few things," she says. "Like the smell in the temple. I think I was in one before, when I was little."

I look at her in surprise, wondering why she didn't say anything to me earlier about it. Min's funny that way – you can never completely read her.

"What?" she asks me. "I know you think you're special with your stupid silence, but guess what? I'm from here too."

I open my mouth to tell her that's not what I was thinking, but Mum gets in first. "Min, I've had just about enough of you being rude to your sister over the last few days," she says. "Apologize right now."

"No!" Min says. "Why is everything always about Sunny? Sunny this, Sunny that. I spend my whole time helping her, telling everyone what she's saying. I'm like her own personal translator, and it's not fair. I always have to go where she wants to go and do what she wants to do. I even put bracelets on for her."

"When?" I ask.

"At your birthday party in the cafe."

She's right – she fastened my new bracelet for me.

"I'm sick of it," she continues. "What about me and what I want to do? I'm a person too."

"We know you are, Min," Dad says. "Lord knows we do.

And I'm sorry. You help Sunny a lot. But she does things for you too."

"Like what?" Min asks.

Dad opens his mouth and then closes it again. He clearly can't think of anything. And right now, neither can I.

"See?" Min says. "I do everything for her. I'm the normal one. She's the freak."

"Min Sullivan, you take that back immediately," Mum says. "Your sister is not a freak. How could you say such a thing?"

"She's just tired, Nadia," Dad says. "You don't mean it, do you, Min?"

Min shakes her head but says nothing.

"Why don't I take you to bed, Minnie Mouse?" Dad says. "Read you some stories? Would you like that? Some Min and Daddy time?"

Min nods. "OK."

Dad carries her through the interconnecting door to our room. When they've gone, Mum says to me, "You know she didn't mean any of that, don't you? Your dad's right – she's just wiped out from all the travelling and the excitement."

"I know." But Min's right – I do rely on her help.

"Sunny, can I ask you something?" Mum says. "Why did you leave your new Monchhichi in the temple the other day? I've been wondering about it."

"We used to go to a temple just like that with our minder, Mama Wei," I explain. "The statue in there was of one of her favourite gods, Mazu, so I left her a present."

"Were you asking Mazu for a favour? Was that it?"

I nod and feel my cheeks go red. Mum can probably guess what I asked for.

Mum smiles at me gently. "Sunny, you know we love you just the way you are, pet. We just want you to be happy, you and your sister. We love you both so much."

"I know. I love you too." I crawl over the bed towards her and give her a hug. I'm aware of exactly how much they love us, which is why I feel so guilty all the time. Mum and Dad deserve a normal daughter, not one like me. Min's right – I am a freak.

# Chapter 17

The following morning – orphanage day – I'm so anxious I can barely eat any breakfast. Min is tucking into a whole plate of pastries – tiny croissants, strawberry tartlets and pains au chocolat – but all I can manage is some fruit salad and a little toast.

I know Mum's worried about me – she keeps looking at me – but I wish she'd stop. I'm not all right. I'm all over the place. I'm petrified and on the verge of tears. A bit of me wants to tell them that I don't want to go because it will bring back too many memories, but another part of me desperately wants to see Shenzhen and the orphanage again. They are a part of who I am, and it feels important to remember that. Also, I want Min to see where we're from. And, yes, I'm still hoping that somehow this trip will make me feel less anxious and unlock my voice.

After breakfast we go outside to wait for the car Dad has ordered, a long black Mercedes. When it arrives, a Chinese man in his twenties in a smart, dark suit climbs out and bows his head to us. "My name is Mr Lin and I'll be your driver today."

Mum and Dad both bow back.

Once our journey is underway, Mr Lin closes the partition between us and the front seats, to give us some privacy, or perhaps because Min keeps asking, "Are we there yet?" every five minutes.

I look out of the tinted window and try not to think about what lies ahead.

"I'm bored," Min whines.

"You can play a game on my phone," Dad suggests.

Min shakes her head and starts bouncing up and down on the seat, her seatbelt straining against her chest.

"Min!" Dad says. "Stay still."

"Why don't I tell you the Collection Day story?" Mum says. "I did promise."

"OK," Min says, settling back into her seat. "I'll start: 'Nadia and John Sullivan wanted a baby very much.'" We've both heard this story so many times we almost know it off by heart.

Mum smiles. "That's right. But unfortunately they couldn't have one so they decided to give a home to two beautiful daughters from China instead. Nadia and Smiles had lived in Hong Kong for many years and loved Chinese culture."

"Especially dim sum and noodles," Min adds. "And moon cakes, like Sunny does too."

Mum laughs. "Yes, they especially liked the food. Anyway, it took almost ten years for Nadia and Smiles to find the right daughters. They had moved into a castle on a small island called Little Bird by then. One day they got a phone call to tell them that their daughters were waiting for them in Shenzhen. So they booked flights immediately."

"You were very excited, weren't you?" Min says.

Mum nods. "Yes, very. We couldn't sit still for two minutes, just like you, Min. The night before we were due to meet you for the first time, we couldn't sleep a wink. We were so worried. Would our new daughters like us? Would we recognize them from their photos? But as soon as we stepped into the offices of the adoption agency, we knew you both instantly. You had a little red ribbon in your hair, Min, and you were holding Sunny's hand so tightly I was worried you'd stop her blood circulation."

In fact, it was the other way round – I was the one squeezing Min's hand – but I've never told my parents that and Min was probably too small to remember.

"Then I knelt down and hugged you both," Mum continues. "And your dad took hundreds of photos."

"You were crying, weren't you, Mum?" Min says.

"Not as much as your dad was," Mum says, blinking quickly. She always cries telling this story.

Dad laughs. "It was an emotional day. And then we had to wait two days until the official Giving and Receiving Day ceremony, when you became our legal daughters."

"It was hard, wasn't it, Smiles? Having to wait like that?" Mum says. "We just wanted to swoop you both up and take you home to Ireland."

"But it was worth the wait," Dad says. "Then two weeks later, after your Irish passports had arrived, we flew back to London and then on to Cork with our new family. It was a miracle." Dad sniffs.

"Still an old softie." Mum leans over and pats his arm. They smile at each other and Mum blows Dad a kiss. The Collection Day story always makes them like this – all soppy and emotional.

"You're the luckiest parents in the world to have not one but two amazing daughters," Min says. "The end."

Min loves that story, and I guess, if I'm honest, I do too. It's so sweet. And now we're going back to the place where it all began.

# Chapter 18

We pull up outside the gates. Inside, three large grey buildings with lots of windows form a U-shape around an open courtyard. There are bright murals on the walls of the buildings and playground games painted onto the concrete ground.

"This is it, Mr Sullivan," our driver, Mr Lin, says. "I'll ask them to open the gates." He gets out of the car and walks towards the intercom on the wall.

"Do you remember this place, Sunny?" Mum asks. "It looks nice. I like the murals on the walls. All the cartoon characters."

"Yes," I say quietly. "The buildings all look the same, but the murals are new."

Memories flow through my head now, like I'm watching a movie: the reception area through the door in the right-hand building where we waited with Mama Wei to be signed in after Papa died, the courtyard where we played, the tall swaying trees of the garden behind the buildings that I could see from my bedroom window.

Min coughs, trying to get attention, and then slides forwards on her seat. "What about me, Mum? You never asked me."

"Not now, Min," Dad says, his voice all serious.

"Sorr-eee," she says huffily, sitting back again. "I think I remember it a bit, in case anyone's interested. We used to play catch over there." She points at the courtyard. "And skipping with a long rope."

"Are you sure, Min?" Mum asks. "You were very small."

"She's right," I say. "We did. Well remembered, Min."

"Thanks." She smiles at me.

I smile back. She was annoying me the whole way here, but now she seems calmer. Like me, she's staring out of the window, taking everything in.

Mum and Dad exchange a glance. They obviously think she was too young to remember anything about the orphanage, but from what she's just said I'm not so sure. She was two when we arrived and just four when we left a year and a bit later. Maybe she is starting to remember things about our life here – first the temple, now this place. China isn't just my story; it's Min's too. It's something we share.

The gates buzz open and Mr Lin gets back into the car. He drives through and parks beside the courtyard. A gang of children runs out of the doorway to the left, towards the car, cheering and laughing.

"Mercedes! Mercedes!" they shout.

A small stern-looking woman in a blue trouser suit rushes out of the reception and tells them to go back inside. The children take one more look at the car before running back inside. We used to do exactly the same thing when people visited – we'd rush out and try to be the first to identify the car brand. It's funny to think they still do that!

Mr Lin opens the passenger door for us and we all step out. The air is warm and humid. Much stickier than back in Hong Kong. Mum takes my hand and holds it firmly. Dad takes Min's.

The woman in the suit walks towards us. She has short black hair and round glasses with thin metal frames. "I am Miss Cheng, director of the orphanage," she says slowly in English. "I would like to welcome you to Shenzhen." She shakes Mum and Dad's hands.

"Thank you," Dad says. "We're happy to be here. And the girls are very excited about visiting. This is Soon Yi and her little sister, Min Yen."

Miss Cheng smiles, but even then she still looks serious. "Good morning, girls. You look very well. I am glad that you have found a bright, happy future with your new family. I was not here when you were with us, but I believe from my records that you were good, well-behaved children."

She reaches over to stroke Min's hair. People do that all the time. It's because she looks so cute and innocent. If only they knew the truth!

"Thank you for letting us visit," Dad says.

"I am pleased to show you around the orphanage," Miss Cheng says. "We often get families visiting and we are always glad to see them. Have you been back to China before, girls?"

Min jumps in immediately to say, "No, this is our first time. The trip was Sunny's birthday present. She's thirteen now."

"Happy birthday, Soon Yi," Miss Cheng says with a nod of her head.

I give her a nod back and a small smile, then stare down at the ground, praying she won't ask anything else or expect me to talk to her.

"Sunny's a bit quiet today," Mum says quickly. "What with the trip and everything. I'm sure you understand."

Miss Cheng says, "Of course." Then she asks where we would like to begin our tour of the orphanage. "Will we start with where the girls used to sleep?" she suggests. "And then I'll show you the rest, the classrooms and the canteen."

We follow Miss Cheng into a building on the right. The hallway is bright and airy, with white tiles on the floor. It is familiar – but it's the smell of damp washing mixed with flowery air freshener that makes me catch my breath and my heart beat faster.

Miss Cheng leads the way up the stairs to one of the bedrooms. Dad and Min are right behind her, me and Mum bringing up the rear. I can feel Mum's eyes on me, so I give her a tiny smile, which she returns.

"The children are resting right now, so we should be quiet," Miss Cheng says, then shows us into a large, white, open room with a whirring ceiling fan above us. There are toddlers in the neat row of cots with metal bars. Some are taking a nap and others are standing up. One of them reaches out her hands when she spots us, just like in my sketch.

I feel as if I've left all my emotions back in the car. I run my fingers over the bars of one of the empty cots. It's so hot in here the metal is warm to the touch. Little Bird is never hot, even in the summer. It took me ages to get used to it, but now I miss the cool air and the gentle breezes.

"So this is where the girls would have slept?" Dad says.

"Min Yen was two when she came to us – is that correct?" Miss Cheng asks.

Dad says, "Yes, that's right. She'd just turned four when we adopted her."

"This is the sleeping area for children up to the age of four," Miss Cheng says. "Min Yen would have slept here to start with, but not Soon Yi. There are different rooms for different ages. Babies, younger children, older children."

"So they were separated?" Mum asks. She sounds surprised.

Miss Cheng nods. "Yes, they would have been separated as soon as they arrived in the orphanage. Unless the siblings are a similar age – it's the policy here."

"I see," Mum says. She and Dad exchange a look.

We visit my old room next, which has small metal beds instead of cots and a view of the trees outside. It hasn't changed much from how I remember it. The walls are still the same creamy colour, but now there are posters over every bed – pictures of animals, Harry Potter, and Pokémon and manga characters. Then we visit a playroom, which has toys in plastic boxes, small tables and chairs, a bookshelf and art materials. There are drawings on the walls and I remember that I used to sit at one of the little tables, drawing pictures, mainly of Min and Puggy. The children in the room look up at us curiously. I remember staring at visitors in just the same way. I used to wonder if they were coming for one of us. Were they someone's new family? I was only six when I arrived, but some of my friends in the orphanage were older and they explained how the system worked – how some children were adopted and others weren't.

We all watched *Charlie and the Chocolate Factory* in here together once. It was dubbed into Cantonese. When Charlie won the golden ticket, one of the boys jumped to his feet and said, "A new family, that's the golden ticket I'd like to win." We all laughed. But he was right. Every child in the orphanage dreamed of finding a new family.

After the playroom, Miss Cheng takes us to the large canteen, which smells so strongly of cooked vegetables that Min wrinkles up her nose until Mum nudges her to stop. "Don't be rude, Min," she whispers.

As we walk out of the canteen, Min drops back to talk to me. She lets Mum and Dad walk on a few steps with Miss Cheng before she says, "The crying babies from my dreams, the ones in the cots – this is where they come from."

I nod.

"Sunny, were we happy here?" she asks softly.

I don't know what to say. Is she ready to hear everything – the happy bits *and* the sad bits? Instead of answering, I pretend I didn't hear my little sister's question.

# Chapter 19

Miss Cheng leads Mum and Dad out of the canteen and towards the front door. It looks like our tour is over, but there's somewhere Miss Cheng hasn't shown us, somewhere important.

I pull Min's arm and, after making sure there's no one around, I whisper, "Min, ask if we can visit the garden. I really need to see it."

"The garden? OK," she says, before darting down the corridor to shout to Mum and Dad.

Miss Cheng looks surprised at Min's request, but she says, "Of course. Follow me, please."

The garden is at the back of the orphanage and it's a lot smaller than I remember. There are a few neat flower beds and a bench in the shade under the old cherry tree. The tree is big – the height of a double-decker bus – and its branches sway in the gentle breeze, dropping pale pink blossom as thin as tissue paper onto the grass. The scent is faint and sweet, like summer. As I breathe it in, what happened here comes back to me in vivid detail...

Puggy's bark.

The tree.

Min.

Falling.

Blood.

I feel like I'm about to faint.

"You're very pale, pet. Sit down for a second," Mum says, gesturing at the bench. "You may be a bit dehydrated. There's water in the car. Let me just tell your dad where we're going." As she walks off to talk to Dad, I notice that Min is staring at me with a funny look in her eyes. She points at the tree, at both of us and then at the ground. She remembers.

I nod slowly, feeling all tight inside. But she doesn't look angry, just a little sad.

Back in the car, I'm gulping down the deliciously cool water from a bottle that Mum found in the special fridge built into the back of the front passenger seat. She gives another bottle to Min, who takes a few sips. Dad stayed to talk to Miss Cheng some more.

"Min, stop playing with the water," Mum says as Min starts flicking water on her face. "I'll be back in a second, girls. Don't leave the car, OK? Stay right here."

"As if we're going to leave the air conditioning," Min says, fanning herself. "It's boiling out there." As soon as Mum's gone, she twists the cap back on her bottle and flops down against the seat. "So tell me about the day we fell out of the cherry tree."

I have to tell Min, it's time. It's part of her story too and she deserves to know the truth. I take a deep breath and then begin. "We were out in the courtyard playing one day and I heard a dog yapping in the street behind the back wall. It sounded just like Puggy – all squeaky and high-pitched."

"Our pet dog?" Min asks.

"Yes. When Papa died, Mama Wei looked after Puggy. I was so sure it was him that I stood on top of the bench in the courtyard so I could climb into the tree and catch a glimpse of him. I missed him so much! But you followed me. I don't know how you did it, but you managed to get into the lower branches. And then you … you fell onto the bench and then the grass."

"Ouch!" Min winces. "I hurt my arm, didn't I?"

"Yes! When I saw you lying there on the grass, not moving, I panicked. I tried to climb down too quickly and I fell too. I knocked myself out. When I woke up, you were gone."

"Where?"

"They'd only taken you to the hospital. You had concussion and a broken arm. But I didn't know that at the time. I was so scared. I thought they'd taken you away because I was a bad sister and hadn't looked after you properly. I'm so sorry you fell – it was all my fault. I was supposed to be looking after you."

"You didn't make me climb the tree," Min says. "Was it Puggy? On the street, I mean."

I shake my head. "No. It was some other dog." Then I ask

her, "When did you start remembering about the accident?"

"Just when I saw the tree. Do Mum and Dad know about me falling and everything?"

"No," I say. "They think you broke your arm in the playground. I've never told them. I didn't want them to think I was a rubbish sister and that I couldn't look after you. I promised Mama before she died that I'd always take care of you, no matter what." But it's Min who looks after me. Like she said yesterday, she does everything for me – and what do I do for her?

Min shrugs. "It doesn't matter about the tree, Sunny. It was an accident. But I want you to start telling me stuff. I want to know about our life in China. Will you tell me about Papa and Mama? And Puggy? All the stories you remember. It didn't mean anything to me before, but now that we've been here it's different."

"I'll tell you everything I can remember, I promise," I say. "And I have some things to show you too, from our old life."

She snuggles against me. "Thanks, Sunny."

I've just started telling her how clever and kind Mama was when Mum opens the door and climbs in. "Dad's just getting directions to your old apartment from Miss Cheng," she says. "He'll be here in a second. You two look very cosy. It's lovely and cool in here, isn't it? Thank goodness for air conditioning. Are you feeling a bit better, Sunny?"

I nod.

"Good." Mum leans back into the seat and closes her eyes.

When she opens them again, she says, "The adoption people never told us about you girls being separated at night here, Sunny. It must have been hard. I know that staying with Min means everything to you."

My numbness cracks and suddenly I start to cry, big hulking sobs that come out of nowhere. It's been such an overwhelming day. Sad and happy and sad again.

"Sunny," Mum says. "I'm so sorry. I didn't mean to upset you. Come here to me." Mum puts her arms around me and holds me tight.

She's still holding me when Dad gets into the car. He must read in my expression that I don't want a fuss, though, because he doesn't ask me if I'm all right. Instead he says, "According to Miss Cheng, the building your family used to live in isn't there any more – but would you like to see the area? Or would you prefer to go back to the hotel? It's up to you."

"We'd like to see the area together," Min says. "Isn't that right, Sunny?"

I nod.

Apart from the tower block – there's a shopping arcade there now – the area is as I remember it. Hand in hand with Min, I show her the playground in the park where we used to play, the temple we used to visit with Mama Wei with its red silk lanterns and sweet incense, and the local dried-seafood shop with the grey cats slinking outside. As we walk around our old neighbourhood, the memories come back thick and fast.

When Dad takes Min inside a shop to buy ice creams, Mum asks, "Do you remember this shop?"

Although we're on a public street and there are lots of people around, I open my mouth, determined to answer her with a simple "Yes". But as I form the shape of the word with my lips, I know it's impossible. I can't force the sound out, even as a whisper. That familiar icy anxious feeling creeps over my body. I swallow and try again. This time it's even worse. My throat is so tight I can barely breathe. My heart sinks. Yet again all my prayers and wishes have come to nothing.

So I give up and nod at her instead.

# Chapter 20

The journey home to Little Bird seems much longer than the journey over. After the nervousness and the excitement of the week, everything drags: the taxi drive to Hong Kong airport, waiting in the departure lounge, the thirteen-hour flight to London. Even though we have the seats that turn into beds again, I only manage to sleep for a few hours. For the rest of the flight I just lie there, thinking.

This time I'm beside Min. When we got on to the aeroplane, she asked if we could sit together. Mum sounded a little surprised when she said, "Yes, of course."

Min's asleep now, as are Mum and Dad, so I grab my sketchbook out of my rucksack and start to draw the next scene in my Lotus Flower and Cherry Blossom story. Lotus Flower is searching the orphanage for her little sister, Cherry Blossom. Strange creatures peep at her through the bars of the cots in a large room. At first glance they look like human babies, but they're not. Some have huge googly eyes and swirling tentacles, like an octopus, instead of hands, others have furry bodies like cats, or are covered in giant fish scales.

They don't talk – they bark or hiss or meow. But Lotus Flower isn't scared. She can see that the monster babies are just as sad and lonely as she is. She touches each one, stroking their heads until they purr or coo. Then she continues her search for Cherry Blossom.

"What are they?" Min has woken up and is peering at my drawings.

I flick to the back of my sketchbook where there is a spare page and write, "Monster babies. It's part of my Lotus Flower story. I'll show you when it's finished." I can't talk on the aeroplane. Most of the passengers are asleep, but the air steward might hear me.

"OK," she says. "They look scary but kind of cute." She yawns. "I'm all tired and stiff."

"Go back to sleep then," I write.

She ignores me. "Sunny, are you glad we went to China?"

I think about this for a second and then nod. It doesn't seem to have helped with my anxiety or my problem with speaking in public. And it was hard, because it reminded me of what we'd both lost. But it also reminded me of happy times: going shopping with Mama, visiting the temple with Mama Wei, playing with Puggy. And the nicest thing of all was sharing some of my memories with Min. I've always felt close to her – she's my only sister after all – but now I feel super close, like we're two peanuts in one shell. I know she'd never admit it, but I think she feels the same way.

"Very glad," I write.

"Me too," she says. "Sunny, can I share your bed?"

I smile and she climbs in next to me, twisting around until her little body is curled against my back.

"Night, Sunny," she whispers.

*Night, Min Yen,* I say in my head.

The Friday after we get back to Little Bird, I'm d̶ ___ ̶ ̶ ̶ ̶ more of my Lotus Flower comic when I hear voices outside. I peer out of the arrow-slit window. It's Mum and Rosie. Mum collected her off the ferry. Even though I like Rosie, the thought of what's ahead makes me nervous. She's here to try another "sliding in" session, but I'm not in the mood. I'm still tired from the trip to China.

Although things have pretty much gone back to normal, there is one thing that is completely different – Min. Every day she asks me new questions about Papa and Mama. I haven't shown her the photos yet. I know it's selfish, but I want to keep them to myself for a few more days. I've decided I'll show her at the weekend, on Sunday maybe.

Rosie and Mum are in the kitchen now. I can hear their voices bubbling up through the cracks in the floor. I put down my sketchbook and roll back the rug so that I can see them and hear what they're saying. Mum is standing in her usual place – leaning against the kitchen counter – and Rosie is sitting on the edge of the table. Dad's there too.

, Rosie asks, "So how did the

ally a special family holiday," Mum says. "The
to see the orphanage and the area they once lived in,
ch is important. But…" She falters. "Oh, I don't know. It's
nothing. I guess … I think we were just hoping for too much."

"What were you hoping for?" Rosie asks.

"For some … change in Sunny, I suppose," Dad says. "We thought that if we visited the orphanage and were able to fill in some of the gaps in Sunny's memory of the place, then it might help her somehow."

"We found out they had to sleep in different rooms at the orphanage," Mum adds. "Maybe that contributed to Sunny feeling so vulnerable and worried. Apparently, Sunny used to sneak into Min's room and sleep on the floor, holding her hand – isn't that sweet? She clearly couldn't bear to be separated from her."

"That is very sweet," Rosie says. "They're obviously incredibly close."

Dad sighs. "I really hoped the trip might change things for Sunny. You know, help her put the past behind her and kick-start her into action in some way. I got the feeling Sunny thought so too. On the afternoon of the day we visited the orphanage, she tried to speak to Nadia – didn't she, darling? It was on a public street."

Rosie leans forward. "Really? What happened?"

"Nothing – she couldn't get the words out," Dad says.

"She did try, though," Mum adds. "That's the important thing. We need to be patient, Smiles."

"Interesting," Rosie says. "And you're right, Nadia – it's great she tried. It means the desire is there. But I'm afraid there are rarely miracles when it comes to anxiety disorders. I did warn you not to look for a quick fix, Smiles."

"I know," Dad says. "I'm an impatient kind of person. I'm not good at waiting. And the whole thing gets to me sometimes. Why is this happening to Sunny? It's not fair. She's been through so much already and she's such a great kid. I guess I just want to jump in and fix things for her."

"I understand your frustration," Rosie says. "You love her and you want her to be happy. Let's give the sliding in a few more weeks. I really do think it's the best way forward at this point. It's been successful with lots of other children I've worked with. Hopefully it will help Sunny too."

I roll the rug back over the crack in the floor then, and sit on the sofa. Poor Mum and Dad. I hate disappointing them all the time. I'll have to try really hard today with Rosie. I want to make them proud of me.

The session with Rosie starts off OK. Mum and Rosie chat at the kitchen table about the China trip, mainly the sightseeing stuff: Kowloon, The Peak, the food, the shops. Goldie is under the table and Rosie reaches down to pet him. Then Rosie turns to me and asks, "Was it strange being back in China, Sunny?"

I nod.

"Did you recognize the streets where you used to live?"

I give a second nod.

"What about the orphanage? Did you remember that, too?"

And another nod.

"Had much changed?"

At this stage, I open my sketchbook to a blank page at the back and write: "There were new murals on the walls." I draw one quickly.

Then I write: "And the cherry tree in the garden was bigger."

Rosie smiles at me gently. "I'm glad you had a good time and were able to remember some happy things from your life there. Your dad said you tried to talk in public. You were brave to give it a go, even if it didn't work out. Very brave. Shall we work towards that goal, Sunny? Getting you to say a few words in public? I believe you can do it."

I shrug. I don't see how I will ever get over my fear, but then I remember the promise I made to myself to try my hardest today, and I nod.

"Good for you," Rosie says. "Let's get started with today's session."

At Rosie's request, Mum sets up a game of Connect 4 on the kitchen table. We decided earlier that we'd play that first, and then Pictionary.

"I want you to show me where I can stand today, Sunny," Rosie says when the game is ready. "I'd like to leave the door open a little, if possible. Would that be all right?"

I feel the familiar tension in my body and I try to breathe through it. After a long while I manage to give a tiny nod.

"Just give it a go," Rosie says. "If it's too much, we can close the door. There's no pressure."

I show her where to stand, halfway down the corridor.

"I'm going to walk with you to the door," she says. "Then I'll leave it open a crack and go back to stand where you asked me to. You go in and play with your mum as if I'm not here. Is that all right, Sunny?"

Even though my hands are shaking, I nod. I don't understand why I'm more nervous today than I was the last time we tried this. Maybe it's because I really, really want it to work now.

When I sit down with Mum to start playing, I can't stop staring at the slightly open door and thinking of Rosie standing just outside it.

"Would you like to be yellow?" Mum asks me. "It's your favourite colour."

I know I'm supposed to say, "Yes," out loud, but it won't come out. So I just nod.

"That's all right, Sunny," Mum says. "No need to talk immediately. Just take it slowly. Try some deep breaths."

I do my milkshake breathing, but I still feel all prickly and nervy. So I close my eyes and picture myself lying in a boat with Min on Monet's water-lily pond. That helps a bit. I open my eyes and give Goldie a rub behind his ears and then try to concentrate on the game again.

Mum slides a red counter into the blue plastic grid. "That's my first go. A red disk right in the middle. Where are you going to go?"

I pick up one of the yellow disks. I open my mouth to say, "Right beside your red," but my throat feels tight and nothing is able to come out.

Mum looks over at the door. "Rosie, can we close the door for a little while?"

"Of course you can if you need to," Rosie says, coming back into the room. "Just take it nice and slowly, Sunny. Baby steps, as they say."

Once the door is closed and Rosie is on the other side of it, we try again. But it's just the same. I try to talk and nothing comes out.

Mum is attempting to stay all smiley and positive, but I can see that she's upset. After half an hour of failure after failure, she goes into the corridor to talk to Rosie.

"I'm sorry," I hear Mum say. "It's not working today. I'm doing my best."

There's quiet for a moment and then a sniff and Rosie says, "Oh, Nadia. Don't upset yourself. This happens sometimes. She's had a lot to take in over the last week, with the trip and visiting the orphanage and everything. Let's go back inside and talk to her."

Mum's eyes are glittering with tears when she walks back into the kitchen, but she still manages to smile at me.

"Sunny, I don't want you to worry about this," Rosie says.

"I'm sure you're still tired after China. We'll meet again when you're feeling a bit fresher, say in a week's time. It's perfectly normal to have off days. Lots of the girls and boys I've helped have them. This doesn't mean it's not going to work."

I nod, but right now I'm not sure I believe her.

That evening, when we're curled up in bed, Min asks me about Rosie. "You were very quiet at dinner," she says. "Mum was too. And you didn't say much about that Rosie lady coming round today."

I tell Min what happened earlier and how disappointed Mum was that I wasn't able to talk today. "Rosie told me that everyone has off days, though," I add. "She said not to worry about it."

"I don't mind if you never talk," Min says, giving me a hug. "You're still my sister, no matter what."

"Thanks, Min."

She snuggles up closer to me.

# Chapter 22

On Saturday morning, Mum walks into the kitchen and says, "Girls, there's something wrong with Goldie's eye. He cut it on a bramble the other day and I think it's infected. I'm going to have to take him to the vet in Redrock. Get your coat, please, Min. Your dad won't be back from London until this evening, so you'll have to come with me."

"What about Sunny?" Min asks.

"Sunny's thirteen now," Mum says. "She can look after herself for a few hours."

Min scowls. "That's not fair. I hate that stinky old ferry. And Goldie always pukes when he's on it."

"That's hardly the poor dog's fault," Mum says. "Come on, we'll miss it if you don't hurry up."

"I'll look after Min if you like," I say.

"Really?" Mum asks me. "Are you sure? It's a big responsibility."

"I've done it before."

"But only when I've gone to the shop or the cafe," Mum says. "This would be all afternoon."

"Please can I stay here, Mum?" Min begs. "I'll be as good as gold. Cross my heart and hope to die." Min crosses herself, but gets it all wrong and manages to hit herself in the face.

Mum laughs. "Min, stop! I don't want to have to deal with two eye injuries. OK, you can stay here if you promise to be good and if you're positive you can cope, Sunny?"

"It'll be fine, Mum," I say. "Trust me."

"I'm bored," Min says, coming into the living room, where I'm trying to read my manga book. Mum's only been gone for half an hour and Min's already moaning.

"Watch telly then."

"Mum says I'm not allowed to when it's nice out, remember?"

"She's not here, is she."

"I suppose." Min picks up the remote control from the coffee table. She channel hops for ages – which is very annoying – before settling on an episode of *SpongeBob*.

After only a few seconds, she switches off the telly and sighs deeply. "I've seen that one before."

"Watch a DVD," I say.

"I've seen all of them, too."

"Do some drawing then."

"Boring."

"Play with Goldie in the garden," I suggest.

"Duh! He's with Mum."

"Jump on the trampoline."

"Boring."

I slam my book closed. "Min! Stop annoying me. Go and do something, anything."

"But there's nothing to do." She starts to jump up and down on the armchair beside me, her feet smashing into the cushions.

I feel like yelling at her, but I know that won't help, so I force myself to be calm as I tell her to get down. "I'm never, ever looking after you again. You're driving me crazy."

She flops down into the armchair, sending tiny dust motes into the air. "You're supposed to be playing with me. You're a rubbish babysitter."

I glare at her. "I'm not your babysitter – I'm your sister. I'm not getting paid or anything. Just get lost, OK."

"Fine." She storms off in a huff.

Next thing, I hear her climbing up the wooden staircase towards the parapets. She's not allowed up there on her own, but, to be honest, I'm past worrying. She can fall over the edge for all I care.

A few seconds later she shouts, "Sunny!"

My heart almost stops – has she fallen and hurt herself? I'm such a terrible sister. I didn't mean what I thought before! I drop my book and run up the stairs to the roof. *Please let her be all right,* I think as I fly through the door and out onto the roof.

Min is jumping up and down excitedly. "Look!" she cries, pointing out to sea. "Whales!"

Min's right – there are three adult whales and a baby whale

swimming off Fastnet Point, which is near Cara Woods on the far side of the island. We take turns watching them through the telescope that Dad set up on the roof. One of the adults is spyhopping – sticking its head out of the water – and it has deep grooves on its underside so it must be a humpback. Cal's mum, Mattie, taught me that when we went out on her sea safari last summer. She's a whale expert, so she told us all about them – how they live and how to tell the different species apart.

"Can we go to Fastnet Point to watch them?" Min begs. "Please? The baby one is so cute, and we'll get a brilliant view from there."

"Fine," I say. At least it will stop her moaning and it would be fun to see a baby whale close up.

"Quick!" she says, hurtling down the steps and back inside. "The whales will be gone by the time we get there if we don't hurry."

"Min! Hold on!" I cry, dashing after her. I stop in the living room to stuff my red sketchbook and a pencil into my pocket in case I get a chance to draw the whales.

I run all the way from the house, but it still takes ages for me to reach the far side of the island. Min must have sprinted, because she's already there, waiting by the tumbling-down deserted farmhouse just in front of Fastnet Point, the fenced-off headland that juts out into the water. Dad says it's been so eroded by the huge Atlantic rollers that it will fall into the sea one day.

"There you are, slowcoach," Min says. "Look, the whales are still there." As we watch, one of the humpbacks shoots water out of his blowhole, high into the air. "Wow!" she says. "Let's get closer." She starts to climb over the wire fence that leads to the Point.

"Min, be careful," I tell her. "We're not supposed to go onto the headland, remember? It's dangerous. Mum will have a fit."

"Careful, schmareful. Don't tell her then." Min reaches the other side of the fence, then looks back at me and grins. "Come on, scaredy-cat. Quick, before that hiker catches up with us." She points up the road. "I don't want to share our whales with anyone else!"

I'm not sure going onto the headland is such a good idea, but Min is darting towards the sea so fast that I'll have to climb over if I'm going to keep up with her. I follow her, picking my way through the wiry marram grass.

Min reaches the end of the land and says, "Hey! Is that another baby whale?" She moves even closer to the edge of the cliff to take a closer look.

"Min!" I say. "Come back from the edge!" I should yell it, but I know the hiker is somewhere near by, so my voice only comes out as a whisper.

Min turns, a grin on her face. "Don't be silly! I'm—"

And suddenly the ground falls away under her feet. She shrieks as she starts sliding down the cliff face.

I dash towards her, my arms outstretched to try to grab

her. But I'm too late, and she's already disappeared. A tiny shriek escapes from me. There are huge jagged boulders at the bottom of the cliff. If Min lands on them, she'll... I can't finish that thought.

Min! Oh, Min.

I creep right to the edge of the cliff, afraid to go too close in case the earth collapses underneath my weight and the debris lands on top of Min. As I peer down at the swirling water below, I hear a groan right beneath me. At least I know she's alive – but I can't see her.

I lie down on the grass and inch my way forwards on my stomach, so I can get a better view down the cliff face. Min is lying on a ledge. She's on her side, with her back facing the sea. One of her arms is trapped under her at a funny angle. There are fallen rocks and earth on top of her chest. There's no way I can reach her. She's too far down.

I hear another moan and then she twists her head to look up at me, blinking some fallen earth out of her eyes. "My arm is sore, Sunny. Everything hurts. And I'm getting c-cold." Her teeth clack together as she speaks.

"I have to go and get help, Min," I say frantically.

She looks panicked. "No! Don't leave me."

Behind me, I hear a voice calling, "Are you all right over there?" There's a tall woman in a green parka standing by the farmhouse, on the other side of the fence. It's the hiker. Thank goodness! I ease myself upright and run over to her. I point at the cliff.

"I'm sorry, I don't really understand," she says. "Can you tell me what's wrong?"

I open my mouth to try, but nothing comes out. I shake my head. Then I point at the cliff again and mouth the word "cliff".

She reads my lips. "The cliff? What about the cliff?"

I mouth "Fall" at her. *Fall. Fall.*

"Fall?" she says. "Someone's fallen? Is that it? Down the cliff?"

I nod furiously. I'm so relieved she understands me.

"I'm coming to help," she says.

I point to the sign on the fence that says DANGER, CLIFF UNSAFE.

"I'll be very careful," she assures me. After climbing over the fence, she walks gingerly towards the cliff edge and I follow her. "Is there anyone down there?" she asks when she's as near to the edge as she dares.

"Yes!" Min shouts. "Me! Help!"

The woman strains her neck to see Min. "You're going to be all right, pet," she says. "We're going to get some help. Just stay very still."

"Is Sunny there?" Min says. "I want Sunny."

"Is that you?" the woman asks me.

I nod.

"She's here," the woman tells Min. "Don't worry. I'm going to ring the emergency services." She takes out her phone and dials 999. When she's finished telling them what's happened and where we are and asked them to hurry, she hangs up, and I point at her mobile.

"You want to use it?" She looks surprised.

I pretend to text with my finger on the palm of my hand.

"Ah, texting, I see." She hands the phone over and I press in Alanna's number and send her a message: *Min fell down cliff – Fastnet Point. Help on way – a hiker found us. She rang 999. Please come! Sunny*

Alanna texts back immediately: *Hang in there. I'm on my way.*

I'm hit by a huge wave of relief. Alanna's coming and so are the emergency services. I lie down on my belly again and crawl forward so that Min can see me. She is so pale. I may not be able to talk to her, but I'm trying to tell her how much I love her with my eyes. Right this second I have never loved her more. My stubborn and brave little sister. But I feel so guilty. She's in serious danger and yet again I haven't been able to call for help.

# Chapter 23

Alanna is running towards us. I'm so relieved to see her. She must have sprinted all the way from the cafe. Her cheeks are bright red and her chest is heaving up and down.

I wave at her.

She waves back.

"Is that your friend?" Liz asks me. That's the hiker's name. She's a primary school teacher from Cork City, she told me. She gave me some water and a chocolate bar to keep me going. She's being very kind. "Is she the one you texted?" she adds.

I nod.

"Sunny!" Alanna says. She climbs over the wire fence and races towards us, slowing down as she gets closer because we're standing right on the edge of the cliff.

"This stupid headland is lethal," Alanna says. "You OK, Sunny?"

I nod again.

She looks at Liz. "I'm Alanna, a friend of Sunny's. Thanks for staying with her."

"I'm Liz. There's a helicopter on the way. Sunny's been

watching the little girl on the cliff like a hawk. Is it her sister?"

"Yes, she's called Min. Is she all right?"

"She's badly hurt," Liz says. "But she's conscious, just about. You can see her for yourself if you look over the edge. Careful, though. The ground is really unstable. It's probably best to lie down."

Alanna lies on the marram grass as Liz suggested and peers down the cliff face. "Oh, Min!" she says. "You poor thing. Can you hear me? It's me, Alanna. The helicopter's coming. They'll airlift you to hospital. Did you get that? Help's on the way. Min!" Alanna tries again, louder. "Stay with us. Don't fall asleep."

Still no reply.

The silence is broken by an engine noise behind us. A jeep is tearing down the road that leads from the village up to the headland.

After wriggling back from the edge, Alanna runs towards the jeep. She scrambles over the fence just as the jeep comes to a stop in front of the farmhouse, sending small stones flying. Leaving Liz watching Min, I follow Alanna. Mattie, Cal's mum, and Shay, one of the local fishermen, climb out of the back of the jeep as I arrive. They're part of the Coastal Rescue team, along with Landy's dad, Bat, who is in the driver's seat. He gives me a little wave.

"Where's Min?" Mattie asks Alanna.

"On a ledge halfway down the cliff. She's just gone unconscious. Sunny and a hiker called Liz did a brilliant job of keeping her awake until now."

Mattie gives me a nod. "Well done, Sunny. Now can I ask you all to stand well back while we set up the ropes?"

Alanna calls Liz away from the cliff. When she has joined us, Alanna says, "They need to act quickly and we'll only be in the way here. Let's sit on the rocks over by the farmhouse. We can see everything from there."

It's a relief to sit down. My legs are wobbly and my heart is racing. I'm so worried about Min that I feel physically sick.

Alanna takes my hand and holds it tight. "She'll be fine, Sunny. Mattie and her team know what they're doing. And the helicopter will be here soon, I promise."

As we watch, Bat batters the fence down with the jeep and then drives a few metres towards the cliff, stopping a good distance from the edge. He kills the engine, jumps out and, with Shay's help, hooks a pulley system to the metal loop at the front of the jeep, while Mattie steps into a harness. Seconds later, Shay and Bat carefully lower Mattie over the edge of the cliff on a rope attached to the pulley system. It all happens remarkably fast.

I stand up to see better. My eyes are glued to the exact spot where Mattie disappeared. A few minutes later, she reappears, but Min isn't with her. Mattie says something to Bat, who runs towards us.

"Min's leg is definitely broken," he tells us. "And maybe her arm too and some ribs. She's unconscious but breathing. Mattie thinks her body has gone into shock. It's too dangerous to try to move her, but Mattie managed to push her further in against the cliff wall and she's also put a safety harness and a rope on her in case the ledge gives way. Now we have to wait until the helicopter arrives. They'll airlift her off the ledge. In fact, I think I can hear it now. I'll fill them in on Min's condition."

Sure enough, as Bat pulls out his handheld radio to make the call, there's a faint whirring noise and I can make out a dark speck in the sky over Redrock. It's getting bigger and bigger.

Bat steps away from the jeep to talk to the helicopter pilot via the radio. I can't hear what he's saying, but I guess he's telling the pilot what has happened and what's wrong with Min. When he's finished, he walks back towards us. "They're going to take her to Cork University Hospital. They're all trained paramedics, so they'll look after her on the flight and make sure she's safe."

I start to cry. Poor Min. Embarrassed, I wipe my tears away with my fingers.

Alanna puts her arm around me and says, "Ah, pet, Min's going to be just fine."

"She's in the best hands, Sunny," Liz adds. "Don't you worry. My sister-in-law's a doctor in that hospital. I'll ring her and make sure they give Min VIP treatment."

I give Liz a nod to say thanks.

The large red-and-white helicopter is hovering over the sea beside the cliff now. It's so close that sand and grit are hitting us in the face. The noise is deafening. I press my hands over my ears to deaden it a little and Alanna and Liz do the same.

The helicopter door slides open and a man in an orange dry suit appears. He's wearing a yellow helmet and there's a harness attached to his body. He's holding what looks like a stretcher in one hand. Another man lowers him down on a winch until he's parallel to the cliff face. Then, like Mattie before him, he disappears over the edge of the cliff.

Waiting for him to reappear is agonizing. But suddenly I see the top of his yellow helmet, then his face, his body and finally the stretcher with Min on it. She's bundled up in a special blanket, so I can't see her face. My eyes tear up again, this time with relief. She's safe!

The helicopter lifts into the air and Min and the man who rescued her are slowly winched up and up. Once they are safely inside, the helicopter powers away, taking Min to the hospital. I watch until it's a black speck in the sky once more.

Alanna hugs me. "Let's go back to the cafe and wait for your mum. And I think we owe Liz a large slice of cake for all her help."

"I wouldn't say no to cake." Liz smiles at me, but I can only manage a tiny smile back. I keep thinking that Mum trusted me to look after my little sister, and now Min's on her way to the hospital. And, if it hadn't been for Liz and Alanna, Min would still be lying on that cliff ledge, because I couldn't call for help. I've let Min down again. She deserves better.

# Chapter 24

Poor Mum gets an awful fright when she hears about Min. Alanna manages to get hold of her on her mobile while she's still at the vet's. Mum arranges for me to get the ferry to Redrock and to meet her there. Goldie will stay with the vet while we travel up to the hospital together in Mum's car to be with Min.

As soon as the ferry docks and I step off, Mum pulls me into a huge hug. "Oh, Sunny. You must have been so scared," she says, stroking my hair. "I rang the hospital. Min's leg, arm and ribs are badly broken and the doctor says she has to stay in for a few nights so they can keep an eye on her. Dad's flying in later. Let's get to the hospital as quickly as possible."

In the car on the way there, Mum asks why I'm being so quiet and I tell her I'm just worried about Min, which is true. But I also can't stop thinking about what could have happened if Liz hadn't come along. And what if she hadn't understood what I was trying to tell her? My sister could be dead now because of me! I can't tell Mum any of this, so I keep it to myself.

"I should never have left the two of you alone like that,"

Mum says, breaking into my thoughts. "Min's too much of a handful. What was I thinking?"

"It wasn't your fault, Mum," I say. "We shouldn't have been on the headland. Min ran on ahead and I couldn't catch her."

"No one can stop Min," she says. "She's a force of nature. Please don't blame yourself, pet. I'm just glad you're both all right."

It's after six by the time we get to the hospital, but the nurse on duty says we're allowed in to see Min for a short visit and that she'll fetch the doctor to talk to us first. The doctor appears a few minutes later – a tiny dark-haired woman with kind brown eyes behind big red glasses. She's wearing a white coat over blue scrubs. She introduces herself as Doctor Kinder and tells us she's Liz's sister-in-law and is making sure Min is getting the best possible care. She says that Min is doing very well and she's given her something for the pain.

When Doctor Kinder says the word "pain", Mum starts to get upset.

"She's a strong wee thing," the doctor says, squeezing Mum's arm. "She'll be back running around in no time at all. Don't you worry."

If the doctor thinks it's strange that I'm not talking, she doesn't mention it – which is a relief.

"Min's just down the corridor," Doctor Kinder says. "Room twenty-six A."

"Can I stay with her overnight?" Mum asks.

"One of the nurses can arrange that, but it will have to be just you, I'm afraid. Siblings aren't allowed."

"My husband's on his way to collect Sunny. They'll stay in a hotel. We're a long way from home."

Doctor Kinder smiles. "That's right – you're from Little Bird. Beautiful place. I've visited with Liz. She loves walking the island. You're very lucky to live there. I have to see a patient now, but I'll be back to check on Min later tonight and first thing in the morning. Let the nurse know if you have any problems."

"Thanks, Doctor," Mum says.

We find Min in a small private room. She's wearing a sky-blue hospital gown and she looks tiny sitting propped up with lots of white pillows in the huge hospital bed. There are two large plasters on her face – one on her forehead, the other on her chin. She has small cuts and grazes scabbing all over her face and arms and her right arm and leg are both in a turquoise plaster cast.

We walk in and Mum closes the door behind us. As soon as I'm sure it's firmly shut, I smile at Min gently and say quietly, "I thought pink was your favourite colour?" I nod at the cast.

"It's blue now," she says, her voice slightly woolly and a little husky, like she's just woken up.

Mum's eyes fill with tears and she kisses the top of Min's head. "Oh, my darling. I'm so sorry."

"Why are you sorry?" Min says. "I'm the one who ran onto the headland. Sunny tried to stop me, by the way. I hope she's not in trouble. It was all my own stupid fault."

"No, Sunny's not in trouble at all," Mum says. "But look at your poor old face and your arm." She gently runs a finger over a black and purple bruise on Min's left arm. "My poor baby."

"Stop fussing," Min tells her. "I'm fine. Tanya said I'm very lucky. My injuries are all on the outside. External, it's called."

Mum looks confused. "Tanya?"

"Doctor Kinder. She said I could call her Tanya. She's really nice."

"You're right – she is nice," Mum says, putting her hand on Min's forehead. "How are you feeling? The doctor said she'd given you painkillers."

"I feel a bit weird," she says. "Kind of tired and achy, and the casts are annoying. I can't really move properly or sit up. But I'm not too sore now, if that's what you mean."

Mum looks relieved. "Good."

Mum's mobile rings then and she whips it out of her bag and answers it. "Smiles, I'm in the hospital with Min. She's absolutely fine. Thank God. I don't think I'm supposed to be on the phone. I'll go outside and ring you back." She looks at us. "I'll be back in a few minutes, girls. Is that all right?"

"Tell Dad I said hi," Min says. "And can you get me some sweets?"

Mum smiles. "Sure. I'll get you both something. I'll be quick."

Once Mum's gone, I say, "Thanks for saying that – about it

not being my fault." My eyes fill up with tears.

"Don't you start going all weepy too. Mum's bad enough." Min shifts around. "Will you move the pillows a bit? I feel like I'm slipping down the bed."

I carefully rearrange the pillows, terrified of hurting her. When I've finished, she says, "Why don't you climb in beside me? There's plenty of room." She pats the mattress to her left.

I kick off my shoes and then snuggle in beside her, taking care not to move her too much. It's comfy. She puts her good hand in mine and I hold it tight.

"Is everyone talking about me on the island?" she asks. "And saying how brave I am? I bet they are." She gives me a slightly wobbly smile.

"Yes," I say. "They're saying you're super brave." And it's true, they are. They're kind on Little Bird. Everyone knows we shouldn't have been on the headland – that it's dangerous – but they haven't said this.

"Stop looking so upset," Min says. "I'm the one who had the accident, not you. Why are you being so mopey?"

"Because it was my fault. I should never have let you near the cliff in the first place. Don't you see? I should have yelled at you to stay back, but I couldn't because the hiker, Liz, was near by. Mum asked me to mind you and you end up in hospital. I couldn't even shout for help or ring the emergency services. If Liz hadn't come along, I don't know what would have happened. This is the second time I've nearly killed you. No third, actually."

Min stares at me. "What are you talking about?"

"The sinking mud at Lough Cara. I should have been watching you. And before that, in China. The cherry tree. I'm supposed to look after you, Min. Always. I promised Mama."

Min looks surprised. "Chinese Mama? When?"

I nod, a lump in my throat. "It was when you were little," I begin. "She got really sick and had to stay in bed all the time. But on the morning of my sixth birthday she got out of bed, even though she was so ill, and made me a special birthday cake. She was a really good cook."

"Like Alanna?" Min says.

"Just like Alanna."

"Where was I?"

"With Mama Wei."

"Am I asking too many questions?"

I smile at her. "Min, you can ask as many questions as you like."

"Really? Cool! How does the moon stay in the sky? How many fish are in the sea? How do whales talk—?"

"Min!"

She grins. "I'm only joking. Go on, I want to hear the rest of the story."

I think for a second, wanting to get it right. "Mama said that she and I were going to have some special time, just the two of us. We spent the whole day together. We climbed into her bed and she read me stories and sang to me. It was wonderful, and she told me how much she loved me and you too, Min.

She said, 'Look after your little sister, Soon Yi. Always. Promise me, whatever happens, you'll never be parted.' And then she gave me some photos. I kept them safe, Min. Would you like to see them?"

"Photos of China? Of our family?"

I nod a little shyly. "I'm sorry I didn't show you before. You never seemed that interested in our life over there and these photos are really special to me."

"China didn't seem real until we went and I started remembering it a little bit," she says. "But now I really care! I want to know everything about it. Can I see the photos? Where are they? At home?"

"No, they're right here." I pull my sketchbook out of my pocket, where I put it all those hours ago, before following Min out to see the whales. The photographs are tucked safely into the back.

I hold the first photograph up in front of Min. It's the one of Mama when she was a little girl, in her red-and-blue silk dress. On the back, Mama had written, in her dark spidery handwriting, "My darling Soon Yi. You are such a good, kind, clever girl. Look after Min Yen for me. Always. Never be parted. I will carry you both in my heart. Mama XXX." But she didn't need to write it down at all. It was already etched onto my heart.

Min gasps. "Who's that girl? She looks just like me." She runs her finger carefully over the photo of Mama.

"It's Mama when she was young," I say.

"Can I see the other photos?" Min asks eagerly.

We pour over my treasured photos together. I tell Min when and where they were taken and how Papa carried a smaller copy of the wedding picture tucked into his wallet.

"Have you shown these to Mum and Dad?" Min asks, after we've studied each one carefully.

I shake my head. "Just you. Can they be our secret for the moment, Min?" I draw a deep breath. "I'm so sorry you got hurt today. I feel like I let Mama down."

"Big sister, you're being crazy. Nothing that's happened to me has been your fault. What age were you when I fell out of that cherry tree?"

I think for a second. "Seven."

"I'm eight – a whole year older – and I'd make a terrible babysitter. And it was me who ran off and got stuck in the mud. Also, it was me who ran off today and fell down that stupid cliff. It was all me. Not you." After a moment, she says, "I'm so tired. Can you sing me the bird song? Until I fall asleep? The one that woman on the plane was singing. I remember it from when I was little."

"Did you really recognize that? It's a Chinese nursery rhyme about a little bird. Mama used to sing it to us. In the orphanage, I'd sneak into your room after lights out and hold your hand and sing it to you. It helped you sleep. I used to fall asleep on the floor beside you."

"Did you stay there all night?"

I nod. "I didn't like leaving you alone."

"And you'd promised Mama you'd look after me."

"Yes. That too."

"See – you did keep your promise." She goes quiet for a moment then asks, "Were you sad? In the orphanage?"

"Sometimes."

"Poor Sunny."

"I missed Mama and Papa, and I used to worry a lot that we'd be separated. I heard the nannies talking, you see. They said no family would want two girls. Every day I worried that you'd be taken away from me too."

"And then Mum and Dad adopted us and you were happy," Min says.

"As soon as I realized they really did want both of us, yes. And now I'm stuck with you for ever." I smile at her.

She pokes her tongue out at me and then smiles back. "Lucky you. I'm sorry all that happened to you in the orphanage. The worrying and everything. And I'm sorry about your talking thing. I shouldn't tease you about it – it's mean."

"That's all right. Not being able to speak annoys me too."

She yawns deeply then and leans back into the pillows.

I start to stroke her hair, just like Mama used to do, and then I sing to her, softly at first, then louder. It's funny because, apart from that time on the plane, I hadn't thought about the little bird song for years. I still remember every word of it, though. I sing it in English, so Min can understand:

*"Once I saw a little bird come hop, hop hop.*

*And I cried, 'Little bird, please stop, stop, stop...'*

*I was going to the window to say how do you do,*
*When he shook his little tail and away he flew."*

Mum comes back into the room in the middle of it. She closes the door carefully behind her. "Don't stop," she says.

When I've finished, she says, "You have a beautiful voice, Sunny. Like a nightingale."

I smile at her. "That's what Alanna calls me. Her little nightingale."

"Where's that song from?" Mum asks.

"School," Min says quickly. "I taught it to her."

Mum's eyes meet mine for a second then she blinks and says, "Oh, I see. Well, Alanna just rang to check how you both were. She sends her love. And your dad's in Cork airport now. He'll be here soon. You two look cosy in that bed. I'd love to climb in with you. I'm wrecked." Mum yawns, setting Min off again.

"Did you find some sweets?" Min asks, talking through another big yawn.

"I did, Min." Mum leans down to adjust Min's blanket. "You can have a few, but after that you need to rest. You've been through an awful lot today."

Min winks at me and I smile back. Mum's right. We have been through a lot today. And not just Min's accident.

"What are you two smiling about?" Mum asks.

For once, we *both* say nothing.

# Chapter 25

The next day, Dad and I head back to Little Bird and Mum stays with Min. Doctor Kinder wants to keep an eye on her, so they won't leave the hospital until Wednesday. I fall asleep on the drive to Redrock. At the harbour, Dad has to rouse me. "Wakey-wakey, sleepy head. You slept the whole way from the hospital. You must have been tired."

I nod. The harbour is quiet, not a person in sight, so I feel comfortable speaking. "Thanks for letting me sleep," I say. "Min usually keeps me awake in the car with her yapping."

Dad grins. "I'm sure she does. But you still miss her, don't you? Even if she is crazy?"

"Yes, it's far too quiet."

He laughs. While he texts Mum to let her know we've made it and to check on Min, I sit up, yawn and stretch my arms, my hands pressing against the top of the jeep. I was tossing and turning all last night in the hotel. I kept having a nightmare that Min was running away from me, towards a black hole. She was always just out of reach and I couldn't call out to save her. I had the same bad dream, over and over again. When I woke up this morning, I knew what I had to do. She's my only sister – it's my job to keep her safe. I can't risk not being able to help her again like yesterday.

"Dad?" I say, before I change my mind. "If Liz hadn't come along when she did and been able to ring the emergency services, then Min might have slid down the cliff and died. I couldn't speak, not even to save my little sister's life."

He sighs and shakes his head. "You're being way too hard on yourself, love."

"I need to be hard on myself," I say. "And I need you to be hard on me too. Mum's way too soft; you're the tough one. I want to be able to speak. I have to, for Min's sake as well as my own. But I can't do it alone. I need Rosie's help. And Alanna's. But most of all I need your help, Dad. Don't let me give up. Make me do it, OK?"

He smiles at me, his eyes glistening. "Sunny, do you have any idea how unbelievably proud of you I am right now? Of course you can do this. You've always been a fighter. I believe in you and I won't let you quit."

"Can you ring Rosie for me, then? Can you ask her to come to Little Bird as soon as she can?"

"Of course." He takes out his mobile and starts looking for her number.

No going back now.

# Chapter 26

I'm in the Songbird Cafe helping Mollie and Alanna to add the finishing touches to the decorations for Min's ninth birthday party. Over the last few days we've made Chinese lanterns in Min's new favourite colour, blue, and a huge HAPPY BIRTHDAY, MIN banner to hang across the outside wall. Min came home from hospital two weeks ago, but she went back in for a check-up this morning. Then Mum took her shopping for a special birthday treat. They're on the ferry now, on their way back from the mainland.

My phone buzzes with a text from Mum: *How's Operation Min going? Our ETA is 5.15 p.m.*

*Almost ready,* I text back. *Wait till you see the decorations.*

*She'll be so excited. See you soon.*

I put the final touches to the huge red heart I've painted on the window overlooking the harbour. Min's name is written, back to front, inside the heart in big sparkling pink letters so she can see it from the ferry.

Alanna's been busy this morning too, baking Min a special birthday cake and making loads of fairy cakes, cookies and sandwiches for the party. Landy and Cal have pitched in as well, helping us blow up balloons and tie bunches of them to every tree, car, boat and lamp-post we can find. Min's in for quite a surprise.

As soon as the ferry is in sight, we all line the harbour walls, waiting for it to dock. We've invited pretty much everyone on the island to the party and loads of them have turned up to greet the ferry. Landy is here with his dad, Bat. There's Cal and his mum, and Mollie, of course. Mollie's great-granny, Nan, has also come along, as have most of Min's school mates, and her teacher. Alanna's inside the cafe, preparing the last of the food. We have a lot of people to feed.

"Here's the ferry!" Mollie shouts.

The girls and boys from Min's school start to wave and cheer as the red boat chugs into the harbour. They all love Min, especially the little ones. Lots of them have brought birthday cards and presents for her. Min will be thrilled – she adores presents!

The ferry staff throw thick ropes over the concrete bollards and the captain reverses the boat until it comes to a stop alongside the steps in the harbour wall.

There are even more cheers when we spot Min. She's sitting in a small wheelchair on the back deck with Mum standing just beside her, holding two huge yellow Toystar shopping bags. Min seems to be giving the ferry staff directions. Dad jumps onto the boat and lifts Min out of the wheelchair. One of the ferrymen carries her wheelchair onto the island while Dad follows, Min in his arms. "Happy birthday, Minnie Mouse," I hear him say.

When they're on dry land, Dad puts Min back into the chair and starts pushing her towards the crowd, and she smiles and waves at everyone like she's the Queen of England. She even poses for photos with some of her school friends.

"This is amazing!" she says. "What a surprise! I had no idea you were planning this for little old *moi*. Now, who wants to give me a birthday hug? Line up if you do. No pushing." She's such a madam. And they do it – everyone lines up, good as gold, to say "Happy birthday" and to give her a hug!

Mollie digs me in the ribs. "Your sister sure loves being the centre of attention."

I smile at my friend. A few weeks ago, Min's behaviour would have annoyed me, but not today. It's just who she is – my crazy little sister.

Mum appears beside me. "All set up for the party?"

I nod.

"Good for you. I'll go inside, see if Alanna needs a hand with anything and get rid of these." She lifts up the bags. "Your sister went a bit mad in the Sylvanian Families department. There's a house and a caravan, plus three new animal families in here."

"Hey, Sunny!" Min shouts as Mum hurries off. "There you are. Come on, Dad, push harder!"

"Yes, Master," he says. But he's grinning, so I can tell he doesn't really mind.

When Min reaches me, she puts her arms out. I bend down and hug her. "Did you do all this? Is it a surprise birthday party?"

When I nod at her, she grins. "Yeah! I love parties. Dad, can Sunny wheel me to the cafe?"

"Of course she can." Dad smiles at me. "Go for it, Sunny."

I wheel Min up the road to where Alanna is waiting in the doorway in her Songbird Cafe apron, beaming at us.

After most of the party food has been eaten, it's time for Min to blow out the candles on her birthday cake. Alanna has asked me to carry it out of the kitchen and I do so very slowly and carefully. It's magnificent – a giant moon cake with MIN written on it in delicate curving pastry and a picture of two intertwined nightingales underneath. "You and Min," Alanna told me earlier.

When I place the cake gently on the table, everyone gasps.

"It's stunning, Alanna," Dad says.

"Beautiful," Mum agrees. They're standing together and Dad squeezes her hand. Mum rests her head on Dad's shoulder.

I point them out to Min by nodding my head in their direction and Min rolls her eyes dramatically. "Mum's going to start crying in a minute," she whispers in my ear. "She's in one of her weepy moods."

I smile at my sister. She's probably right.

Min blows out her candles – unlike me she doesn't need any help – and then screws her eyes shut to make a wish.

When she opens them, she winks at me.

"What did you wish for, Min?" Mollie asks.

"My lips are sealed," Min says, pretending to zip them shut. "It won't come true if I tell you."

Dad catches my eye. He tilts his head and mouths "OK?". I nod back at him. He can tell how nervous I am right now.

Alanna pulls me aside. "Are you sure about this, Sunny?" she asks gently. "It's not too late to change your mind."

I shake my head, determined. It's going to be all right. Min's here, my mum and dad are here, and Alanna's here.

She squeezes my shoulder. "I'll be right beside you. You can do it. I believe in you and Rosie believes in you and your dad believes in you. You just need to believe in yourself, Sunny. You're a remarkable girl. Don't forget that. And even if this doesn't work out, you're still amazing for trying."

I nod. Even thinking about what I'm about to do is frightening, so I concentrate on picturing my happy scene to soothe my nerves. Just like Rosie taught me. I'm floating on Monet's water-lily pond in a little wooden boat, Min by my side. All is peaceful.

*Keep calm,* I tell myself. *I can do this. For Mum and Dad and Min. And for me. It's time.*

"Now?" Alanna asks.

I nod.

Alanna picks up a glass and dings it with a fork. Everyone stops chatting and looks at her.

"Thanks for coming to the cafe for Min's surprise birthday

party," Alanna says. "And now Sunny has something that she'd like to say."

"But she can't talk," Conor, a boy in Min's class, says loudly. His mum shushes him. But I know it's what everyone else is thinking. Mum and Min are staring at me in amazement.

I open my mouth to speak, but my throat is too dry. Alanna hands me a glass of water and I take a sip and try again.

"Hap … hap…" I begin, my voice as breathy as the wind.

"She said something," Conor says.

"If you don't be quiet we're going home right now, young man," his mum hisses at him. But I don't mind – because he's right. I did say something. And maybe I can say more. Maybe I really can do this! A wave of adrenaline surges through my body. The room has gone completely silent and I can feel everyone's eyes on me. Mum is holding on to Dad as if she's about to fall over. But I concentrate on Min's hopeful, shining face and block everything else out.

I start again, and very slowly, taking a deep breath between each word, like Rosie taught me, I say, "Happy … birthday … Min."

That's all I can manage. Like Mum, I think I'm about to collapse.

"You spoke!" Min squeals. "Sunny, you did it!"

Everyone claps and cheers. Mum and Dad rush towards me. As predicted, Mum's crying. She throws her arms around me and kisses me. When she finally lets go, Dad says, "Attagirl, Sunny. I knew you could do it. All the hard work paid off."

"Hard work?" Mum says. "What do you mean, Smiles?"

"Sunny's been working on that sliding in exercise with Rosie and Alanna for the last two weeks," he explains. "It was Sunny's idea. She's been incredibly brave, trying to do this on her own without you. We didn't want you to be disappointed if it didn't work. But as you can see, it did. And Rosie says Sunny is making remarkable progress."

"I still can't believe it," Mum says, tears rolling down her cheeks. "I thought she was helping Alanna in the kitchen. I never dreamed… It's all so…" She starts sobbing.

"Oh, Nadia, come here to me," Dad says. He pulls her into a hug.

"I'm just so happy," Mum says. "It's a miracle."

"Ahem!" Min appears beside us, Alanna pushing her wheelchair. "What about my leg and arm? I'm the miracle for surviving that fall. And it's my birthday party, remember?"

"Now that Sunny's found her voice, you may need to get used to sharing the limelight, Min," Alanna says.

Min rolls her eyes. "I guess." Then she grins at me. "But I don't mind. She's the best sister in the world."

# Chapter 27

That evening we have a birthday dinner for Min. Dad is cooking Chinese chicken noodles in a wok on the stove and afterwards we're having vanilla ice cream and strawberry jelly – Min's favourite dessert. She loves poking the jelly with her finger and making it wobble. Dad's just having the ice cream on account of his slimy food phobia.

"Girls, will you set the table?" Mum asks.

"I'll do it," I say. "Min's the birthday girl. Besides, she's only got one working hand." I take the cutlery out of the drawer and start laying four places.

"Thanks, Sunny," Min says.

Mum smiles too. "It's so peaceful around here when you two get on."

"But it's a bit weird," Dad adds. "Almost too quiet."

Goldie gives a bark from under the table.

"I think Goldie agrees, Dad," I say. "But we don't have anything to fight about today. Do we, Min?"

"Apart from you stealing the show at *my* birthday party?" She pretends to look huffy, but I can tell she doesn't mean it.

"And you've never done that at *my* birthday parties?" I ask her.

She grins. "Never."

Mum puts glasses and a jug of water on the table and asks Dad if he's ready.

He nods. "Ready," he says, and serves the noodles onto four plates. They smell spicy and delicious. When we've all sat down to eat, Mum says, "Go on, Smiles, I can't wait."

"What is it, Mum?" Min asks.

"We have an extra present for you, Minnie Mouse," Dad says. He reaches into the back pocket of his jeans, takes out a slightly squished envelope and passes it to Min.

She opens it and squeals. "No way! Disneyland in Paris. Thanks, Dad." Min blows him a kiss.

"It was Sunny's idea," he says.

"I know how much you want to go, Min," I say. "Happy birthday, little sister."

She gives me the biggest grin ever.

Later, when we're lying in bed, Min snuggles up to me.

"It's been the best day ever, hasn't it?" she says. "Apart from the day Mum and Dad adopted us. That was the number-one best day."

"Yes. That was a pretty special day, all right."

Min drifts off to sleep after that, but I can't. In the end I climb out of bed, making sure not to wake her, take my red sketchbook off my desk and then walk down the corridor to Mum and Dad's room.

Mum's sitting up in bed, reading a book. Dad must be upstairs on his computer, working.

"Everything OK, Sunny?" Mum asks.

"I want to show you something," I say.

"Jump in, then." She pats the bed beside her. I climb in and she puts her arm around me. I can feel the solid warmth of her body through my pyjamas. It gives me the courage to take my China photos out of my sketchbook and arrange them on the duvet in front of me.

She stares down at them and then back at me. "I was wondering when you were going to show me these."

"You know about my photos?"

"Yes. They were in a little bundle in your orphanage clothes. I figured you'd tell me about them when you were ready. The little bird song – the one you sang to Min when she was in hospital – that's from China too, isn't it? I remember it from my teaching days."

I nod. "Mama used to sing it to us. I'm sorry – I shouldn't have let Min lie to you like that."

"She was just protecting you, pet. You've always been close, but since China you seem even closer and that makes me really happy. So, tell me more about Puggy." She touches her finger to Puggy's nose in the photo.

As we talk about the pictures, I find myself telling her everything: about how I felt when Mama and then Papa died, about the day Mama Wei took us to the orphanage, about the cherry tree accident and my fear of being separated from Min.

"When she was in the hospital, you thought they'd taken her away from you for ever?" Mum asks.

I can't get the words out, so I just nod.

"Oh, Sunny. You must have been terrified. Is that why you were so nervous when you first met us? You thought we only wanted one of you?"

I nod again.

Mum hugs me close to her. "We definitely wanted both of you. With all our hearts. We asked for two little Chinese daughters and we got the best girls in the world. Thank you for sharing your photos with me, Sunny. It means a lot. Has Min seen them?"

"Yes. I showed them to her in the hospital. I'll share them with Dad next. And then Alanna and Rosie and some of my other friends. I'd like to wait until I can tell them all about the photos properly, though – talk about them, I mean – and about China and everything."

"Your dad would love to see these. And I'm sure your friends would too. But all in your own time, pet. No rush." Mum's eyes start to well up.

"Oh, Mum!" I say. "Not again."

"They're happy tears," she says. "Very, very happy tears."

"You're such a softie." I give her a big hug.

# Chapter 28

The morning after Min's party, I wake up early, and after breakfast I stay in my room to work on the final scene of my Lotus Flower and Cherry Blossom story. I draw Lotus Flower finding her sister sitting under an enchanted fairy tree that is frothy with pink blossom. They hug each other and are immediately transported back to their own fairy world, where they are reunited with their fairy family.

The very last comic cell shows their dog, Firecracker, wagging his tail and saying, "There's no place like home." I got that from Dorothy in *The Wizard of Oz*. It's a film I watch with Mollie a lot – it's one of our favourites.

Later that afternoon I walk down to the cafe to see Alanna. She's in the kitchen, mixing pastry in a big ceramic bowl. She puts down the wooden spoon and wipes her floury hands on her Songbird Cafe apron before giving me a hug.

"I'm making moon cakes," she says, smiling. "The birthday cake was such a hit at Min's party that people have been asking for them. I've created my own special recipe.

I'll make some extra for you and Min."

"Thanks." It slips out easily, like I've always been able to talk to Alanna. My voice is still quiet and my sentences are short, but I can't tell you how excited and relieved I am to be able to use my voice, even in a small way. Rosie says we have a long way to go yet. She has every confidence that I'll be speaking fluently by the end of the year, though. "Baby steps," she says. "Take it one day at a time, Sunny."

Alanna smiles. "I still can't get over hearing you speak, little nightingale. Do you know why I call you that?"

I shake my head.

"Because nightingales have beautiful voices. And I always knew you'd have a beautiful voice one day. How's that mad sister of yours doing?"

"Good. She sent you this." I hand Alanna the "thank you for my party" card that Min made for her, with my help. Surprisingly, it was Min's idea. Mum usually has to talk her into writing any kind of thank-you letter, but this time Min insisted.

There's a picture of the cafe on the front – I drew it and Min coloured it in – and inside Min has drawn dozens of hearts and kisses around Alanna's name with her favourite glitter pens.

"It's beautiful," Alanna says. "Tell her I love it."

"And this" – I pass over the large tube of paper I've been clutching – "is for helping me."

She unrolls it and gasps. "Sunny, is this your work? It's extraordinary. It must have taken you hours." It's a drawing of a fairy girl. She's tall and willowy, with emerald-green eyes and slightly pointy ears. Her long brown hair is in two plaits, interwoven with ribbons. She's wearing a floaty pale-blue dress and there are delicate white wings on her back. There's a faint golden aura around her head, like a ray of sunlight shining through the trees.

"It's you," I say.

She gazes at my drawing. "It's the most beautiful thing anyone's ever given me. I'm going to get it framed and hang it on my bedroom wall. That way I can see it every night before I go to sleep and every morning when I wake up."

I beam at her.

"Now, would you like to make a wish on the moon-cake mix?" she asks.

"No, thank you," I say.

Alanna looks surprised for a moment, then she smiles.

"I don't need to make any more wishes," I explain, my voice coming out clear and strong. "All of mine have already come true."

# Five things you might not know about me

## by Sunny Sullivan

1. I love drawing more than anything else in the world.
Picking up a pencil and sketching makes me happy.

2. I love dogs. We had a black pug called Puggy in
China. Then came Woody, and now we have Goldie,
a golden Labrador.

3. My favourite colour is a golden, happy yellow.
Sunny yellow, like me!

4. My favourite artists are Monet and Frida Kahlo.
I love looking at paintings – good ones make me feel
like I'm in the painting too.

5. If I could have any super power, it would be the
power to change into any animal I wanted.
So if I wanted to spy on people, I could be a tiny fly.
If I wanted to fly, I could be a mighty eagle.
If I wanted to swim, I could be a dolphin.
Wouldn't that be an amazing super power?

# My top five graphic novels and manga

## by Sunny Sullivan

1. *Smile* by Raina Telgemeier
Based on the author's own life as a teenager, it is about family and friendship.

2. *Sister* by Raina Telgemeier
I like this one cos it's about sisters. My little sister, Min, drives me crazy sometimes. But I love her really!

3. *Adventure Time*, created by Pendleton North
I love the illustrations of Finn, his dog, Jake, Princess Bubblegum and Marceline the Vampire Queen in the land of Ooo, and the stories are really funny.

4. *Vermonia* by Yoyo
Great manga with lots of action.

5. *It's a Magical World: A Calvin and Hobbes Collection* by Bill Watterson
My dad loves the Calvin and Hobbes stories – about a boy and his toy tiger who comes to life. He gave me this book for Christmas. Reading it makes me laugh!

# Recipe for the Songbird Cafe Top Hats

## by Alanna D'Arcy

Top Hats are great for serving at birthday parties. Sunny and Min had them at theirs. I hope you like them too. They're easy and fun to make!

### Ingredients (*makes 12-14*)

1 large bar of good quality milk chocolate
1 packet of marshmallows
1 packet of Smarties or Jelly Tots
1 tub of Hundreds and Thousands
Small paper cases (sweet cases)

**Instructions**

1. Melt the chocolate, either on the stove
or in the microwave. Ask an adult to help you
with this and be careful.
2. Place a teaspoon of melted chocolate into each
paper case, filling it up halfway.
3. Put a marshmallow on the chocolate.
4. Put a drop of melted chocolate on each
marshmallow and press a sweet into it. Sprinkle the top
with hundreds and thousands. Leave to set.
5. Eat – delicious!

# Interview with Sarah Webb

## (author of The Songbird Cafe Girls)

**1. How long did it take you to write *Sunny Days and Moon Cakes*?**
About a year, on and off. I did a lot of research into Sunny's condition – selective mutism: reading books, watching documentaries and talking to mums of children with the condition. It's something lots of children have, so I wanted to get it right.

**2. Have you ever been to China, where Sunny and Min were born?**
Yes. In 2013, I spoke at a book festival in Hong Kong and visited lots of Chinese schools on Hong Kong Island and on the mainland. It was an amazing experience – one I'll never forget. It's such a magical, special place.

**3. How did the trip inspire the book?**
Lots of the places Sunny and Min visit on their trip to Hong Kong were inspired by real places. The temple with the huge incense coils, the shop full of Hello Kitty and Monchhichi dolls, the cats, the blossom on the cherry trees, the dried-seafood shops, the food, the smells, the noises, all came from

real things I'd seen or experienced in China. Sadly, we didn't stay in a hotel with a Jacuzzi like the girls did!

## 4. Where and when do you write?

I write at the small, very old desk I used to do my homework on, in the corner of my bedroom. It's like an old friend at this stage. I write mostly in the mornings when my children, Amy and Jago, are at school.

## 5. Do you have any tips for young writers?

Yes! Number one: practise. Write as often as you can. Keep a diary and write down all your thoughts. Carry a notebook and jot down ideas or snippets of dialogue you overhear or funny stories people tell you. Write short stories or poems or reviews of movies and books you like. Keep writing no matter what.

Number two: read. Not just fiction, but all kinds of things – history books, comics, factual books about nature and the world. The more you know, the more you'll have to write about.

Number three: never give up. If you want to be a writer, follow your dream.

## 6. We have loved reading about Sunny and Min. Are there any more books set on Little Bird?

You can read Mollie's story in *Mollie Cinnamon Is Not a Cupcake*. And in *Aurora and the Popcorn Dolphin*, a new girl with a very special talent arrives on the island.

# Acknowledgements

Writing a book is a strange business. After careful thinking, planning and research, you sit down at an empty screen and gradually your fingers start to type and a story begins to unfold. After you've written the first version (the first "draft") all the hard work really begins: crafting the book and making it the very best it can be.

Sunny's story was a difficult one to tell and I wanted to get it right, so there were many different versions of this book. Each version was lovingly edited by my super-smart and kind editor, Annalie, ably assisted by Emily.

Maria gave it a glowing cover (don't you just love Sunny's headphones) and Jack created the fantastic map of Little Bird. Thanks must also go to Team Walker Books, especially Conor, Paul, Gill, Victoria, Jo and Heidi. And to Philippa and Peta, my lovely agents.

Simone Michel gave me such help and encouragement, and Maggie Johnson's book *The Selective Mutism Resource Manual* was invaluable. If you want to know more about selective mutism, it's a brilliant read, full of wisdom. I'm very grateful for Maggie's kind words about my book at just the right time and for inspiring the "sliding in" scenes in the story.

My friend in Hong Kong, Louise Law, was most helpful with Chinese details and I must thank her for inviting me to her literary festival in 2013. Sunny's story was coloured by that extraordinary trip.

I'd also like to thank most sincerely the amazing gang at the Irish Coast Guard at Waterford, who arranged for me to fly in their rescue helicopter, especially Keith Carolan (and hi to his daughter, Aishling), Declan Geoghegan and Ger Hegarty. It was a remarkable experience and made the cliff-rescue scene in the book truly come alive. And thank you to Philip Stanley for putting me in touch with the team.

And finally I'd like to thank you, my reader, for picking up Sunny's story. Books only truly come alive when they are read. I'd love to hear from you, so do drop me a line. sarah@sarahwebb.ie.

Yours in books,
Sarah XXX

**Sarah Webb** worked as a children's bookseller for many years before becoming a full-time writer. Writing is her dream job because it means she can travel, read books and magazines, watch movies, and interrogate friends and family, all in the name of "research". She adores stationery, especially stickers, and is a huge reader – she reads at least one book a week. As well as The Songbird Cafe Girls series, Sarah has written six Ask Amy Green books, eleven adult novels and many books for younger children. She visits a school every Friday during term time and loves meeting young readers and writers. She has been shortlisted for the Queen of Teen Award (twice!) and the Irish Book Awards.

Find out more about Sarah at www.SarahWebb.ie or on Twitter (@sarahwebbishere) and facebook.com/sarahwebbwriter.

Don't miss the next book about
the Songbird Cafe Girls

AURORA
AND THE
POPCORN
DOLPHIN